BEWARE!
DO NOT READ THIS
BOOK FROM
BEGINNING TO END!

All right! You won a contest! Your prize is a trip to a horror writer's convention at Twisted Tree Lodge.

The only problem is, the horror at the lodge is all too real —

Like that strange howling you keep hearing. And the sinister man in the black cape. And what about the strange manuscript pages you keep finding? Pages that seem to predict your future!

Can you learn the secret of Twisted Tree Lodge — before it's too late?

This scary adventure is all about *you*. You make the choices. And you decide how terrifying the scares will be!

Start on Page 1. Then follow the instructions at the bottom of the page. If you make the right choices, you'll have an excellent adventure at Twisted Tree Lodge. But if you choose badly — BEWARE!

SO TAKE A DEEP BREATH. CROSS YOUR FINGERS. AND TURN TO PAGE 1 TO *GIVE YOURSELF GOOSEBUMPS*!

READER BEWARE —
YOU CHOOSE THE SCARE!

Look for more
GIVE YOURSELF GOOSEBUMPS adventures
from R.L. STINE:

R.L. STINE

GIVE YOURSELF

Goosebumps®

THE WEREWOLF OF TWISTED TREE LODGE

AN
APPLE
PAPERBACK

SCHOLASTIC INC.
New York Toronto London Auckland Sydney

A PARACHUTE PRESS BOOK

ISBN 0-590-46306-3

Copyright © 1998 by Parachute Press, Inc. All rights reserved. Published by Scholastic Inc. GOOSEBUMPS is a registered trademark of Parachute Press, Inc. SCHOLASTIC, APPLE PAPERBACKS, and logos are trademarks and/or registered trademarks of Scholastic Inc.

12 11 10 9 8 7 6 5 4 3 2 1   8 9/9 0 1 2 3/0

Printed in the U.S.A.   40

First Scholastic printing, November 1998

"Last stop, Twisted Tree Lodge!" The bus driver's booming voice startles you. You must have dozed off.

"Finally," you mutter under your breath. Last stop? The *only* stop is more like it. And the bus driver didn't need to yell. You're the only passenger on this freezing hunk of junk.

You open your duffel bag and toss in the video game you've been playing. It lands on top of a couple of candy bars, a rubber-band ball, and your short story, "The Revenge of the Werewolves."

This is the story that won first prize for Best Horror Story at the school book fair. As the winner, you get an all-expenses-paid trip to a horror story convention at Twisted Tree Lodge. All the best-known horror writers will be there.

Cool. Except for one thing.

You didn't write the story.

Go to PAGE 2.

Just seeing the story makes you feel guilty. You found it in the school garbage bin. As a joke, you wrote your name at the top. You never even read it. Then you lost it somewhere.

The next thing you knew, your name was being announced as the winner of the Best Horror Story contest! Now here you are, riding along the dark cliffs in a snowstorm to claim your prize. The prize you know isn't really yours.

"This is the end for you," the bus driver announces. He brings the bus to a jerky stop.

Did he have to put it that way? You grab your bag and get off. The bus pulls away, leaving you in a cloud of exhaust.

An enormous, gnarled tree looms ahead of you. You spot a banner hanging from the lodge behind it: WELCOME TO TWISTED TREE LODGE. HOME TO HORROR.

Go to PAGE 3.

"Some welcome," you mutter. "Where is everybody?"

A movement in the bushes startles you. A man dressed in black emerges from the shadows. His black hat is pulled down so low you can't see his face. He carries a black briefcase.

Suddenly, his case flies open. Manuscript pages pour out.

"Oh, no!" he cries. A gust of wind swirls the papers around the grounds of the lodge. "The story!" the man exclaims.

Several pages land at your feet. You kneel down and scan them. They seem to be part of a horror story. Is the man in black one of the famous writers you're supposed to meet?

You glance up and discover the man has vanished. "Hey!" you call out. "You forgot your..." Then you shrug. He's already gone.

You look at the top page of your crumpled pile. It's the title page of a story called "The Revenge of the Werewolves."

Your mouth drops open. That's the name of your winning story! Well, your *fake* winning story. You continue reading.

A kid wins a contest. Just like you. And arrives at a lodge. Just like you! It's all here. Even the man and the briefcase.

You gasp as the realization hits you.

You are actually living out this story *right now*!

Turn to PAGE 62.

4

You and Corey scoot under the bed. Blecch. These ghouls are lousy housekeepers. A thick layer of dust covers the floor.

The door swings open and Maria Canto enters. "Are you all right, dearie? Sometimes transformations can be upsetting."

You watch her feet stop in front of the bed.

"Dearie?" she calls.

Your nose wrinkles. Oh, man. Your allergies. You don't know how long you can stand it under the bed with all this dust.

"Come out, come out, wherever you are . . ." She opens the closet.

Oh, no! You can't hold back.

"Ah-chooo!" That was one major sneeze.

"Who's that? Who is under that bed?" Maria Canto rushes over to you.

Well, duh. Who does she think it is?

"Oh, these full moons get me all jittery," she complains. "Now speak. Who is hiding under that bed?"

You sneeze again. Louder. "Aaaaahhhh-chooooo!"

"Nobody here but us dust bunnies!" Corey exclaims.

Turn to PAGE 9.

"Out!" Canto shrieks. "Get out now!"

You hear the front door of the lodge creak open. You hear Maria Canto, "Grim" Grimsy, and Peter Wilkes screaming and shouting as they dash out of the lodge. Their voices grow fainter and fainter.

"They're gone," Corey declares. He shakes his head. "Too weird."

"Freaked out by some dust." You put on your coat and pick up your duffel bag. "Let's get out of this place."

You and Corey gather your belongings and begin the long, slow trip down the mountain. You think over everything that has happened. A broad grin spreads across your face.

"What are you smiling about?" Corey asks.

"Not only did we save ourselves from a pack of ghouls," you explain, "but I have a great new excuse to never clean my room!"

THE END

6

"Escape?" you repeat. "Why?"

The boy shimmies down the sheet. He drops down beside you. "Something weird is going on here," the boy tells you. "This whole place is crawling with creatures . . . scary, horrible creatures!"

You raise an eyebrow. This kid has some imagination. "Why do you say that?"

He glances around nervously. "I won a contest," he replies. "And when I arrived, a strange woman locked me in a room. I heard her blast some guy for having too many characters in his story. She said he had to get rid of a couple of them."

"That doesn't sound very suspicious," you protest. Although it's weird that the woman locked him in. That's not normal.

The boy glares at you. "Yeah? Well, then this guy barged into my room. I tried to run out. He told me to stay put until the other character arrived. Then he'd take care of both of us. And when he grabbed me, I noticed his fingers looked like claws!"

"Claws?" you repeat. "What did this guy look like?"

"Like that!" the boy exclaims, pointing up at the lodge.

Leaning out the window is the same man who dropped the manuscript pages. The man in black!

Go to PAGE 110.

The other side is blank! "But ... but ...," you stammer. There were words on the other side. Just moments ago! This is freaky.

You flip the page back over. Your eyes widen in shock. Now the other side is blank too! What is going on here?

CLICK. WHAM! The door slams open. The man in black stands in the doorway. "Good," he declares. "I see you have some notepaper handy. Here's the deal. I wrote too many kids into this story. You were the last one to arrive. Anyway, I need to cut a few. But we want to be fair. We're asking each kid to write a list of ten reasons you should be allowed to continue as a character."

Your head spins. What is this guy telling you? That your life depends on some stupid top-ten list?

Yup. That's exactly what he's telling you.

Turn to PAGE 136.

"This is a prizewinning story?" You start to laugh. "*I* could have written something better than this!"

So much for finding out the future. No way did you *really* believe the story was predicting the future. All that stuff in the beginning was just a coincidence.

Nah, you think, this story could never have won the contest. It's too lame. Writers being hunted by their own creations? Readers facing the same horrors? Too weird. No one would believe it. Still, the man in black with the briefcase will probably want it back.

You climb the steps of the huge lodge. The door is locked.

You lift the heavy door knocker. "Whoa," you exclaim. The knocker is an intricately carved wolf's head. It looks so real, almost like it could bite you.

As you wait for someone to open the door, you spot the man in black. He slinks through the hedges and turns a corner.

"Hey!" you call after him, holding up the manuscript pages. But he doesn't seem to hear you. Should you go after him? Or should you first let the contest people know you're here?

If you go into the lodge first, turn to PAGE 10.
If you run after the man in black, turn to PAGE 40.

You stare at Corey. *Dust bunnies?*

He shrugs.

"Dust bunnies? No, not dust bunnies!" Maria Canto shrieks in horror. She races from the room, screaming.

Amazing. A centuries-old, deadly vampire totally freaked out by ... *dust bunnies.*

What are dust bunnies, anyway?

That's the first thing you ask Corey when you crawl out from under the bed.

"That's what my mom calls clumps of dust that pile up under furniture," he explains.

You hear Maria Canto screaming downstairs. "Run!" she shrieks. "Like you've never run before!"

"What's wrong?" You recognize Wilkes's voice.

"It's too horrible," Maria moans. "We have to get out of here. NOW!"

You and Corey stare at each other, listening.

What are you going to do?

Find out on PAGE 5.

You decide to go into the lodge. You shove the loose pages into your duffel bag. You reach for the wolf-head knocker to try knocking again. To your surprise, the eyes on the wolf open!

It's alive!

No, it's not, you scold yourself. Someone is looking out from the other side of the door. Checking you out.

You hear a lock being unbolted. The heavy door creaks open slowly. You step into a huge, rustic-looking lobby. The room is old, damp, chilly, and run-down.

It's also empty.

"Hello?" You gulp. If no one is here, who let you in?

This is getting weirder by the minute.

You cross to the front desk. A silver bell sits on the counter. You hit it. The little *DING* sounds cheerful in the gloomy surroundings. Maybe it will bring someone. You are about to hit it again when someone behind you grabs your arm.

"Don't ring that bell!"

Turn to PAGE 52.

Your heart pounds as the footsteps come closer and closer. You read Side One first.

"Two winners arrive on the same dark day.
One chooses to leave, one chooses to stay.
The one who stays shall stay for good.
If the kid read Side Two, the kid never would."

What the . . . ? Is this some kind of warning? You flip the paper over. And gasp!

Flip to PAGE 7.

Corey takes a peek. "You're right!" he gasps. "He's not a man anymore. He's . . . he's turning into a wolf!"

You watch in horror as the wolf-man throws back his head to howl. By the light of the full moon you see patches of fur sprouting on his cheeks and forehead.

Your heart pounds hard as the truth sinks in. Every word Corey said was true! There *are* werewolves here. And they're after you! It seems impossible, but there he is. You can even smell him.

The wolf-man seems more animal than human now. His eyes have an evil gleam as he scans the area. Now he and the dog both sniff the air.

"They're going to find us!" you whisper to Corey.

"Maybe he just wants the manuscript pages," Corey suggests. "If we dump them here and run, maybe he'll leave us alone."

"We need them to get out of these woods, remember?" you argue. "The manuscript said the pages will help us."

"You don't believe all that stuff, do you?" Corey asks.

"I'm not sure what I believe," you answer. "I didn't believe in werewolves, either."

If you decide to leave the manuscript pages for the wolf-man, go to PAGE 58.

If you decide to take them with you, go to PAGE 81.

"He sees us!" you cry.

Corey scurries down the sheet. You slide halfway, then jump to the ground. You follow Corey across the lawn.

As you run you find more loose manuscript pages. You snatch them up, stuffing them inside your parka. You reach the edge of the woods and stop. You stare at a battered sign. It reads: LOST WORLD WOODS: ENTER AT YOUR OWN RISK.

A page falls out of your parka. You pick it up and read it to Corey:

> "'Beware the creatures of Lost World Woods.
> They await you at every turn.
> Only these pages will do you some good.
> Read them and try to learn
> How to defeat your evil foes
> Whose mission it is to take you.
> The choices you make from this moment on
> Are the ones that will make or break you.'"

"Uh-oh," you breathe. "Trouble. Should we go into the woods?"

"It's either the woods or him," Corey says, pointing to the man running toward you.

If the woods seem less scary than the man, go to PAGE 39.

If the man seems less scary than the woods, go to PAGE 54.

14

You duck under the oak desk. You notice it has carved paws for feet. You sit hunched in the small space, holding your breath.

The footsteps pass the room. And keep going. Soon, you don't hear them at all.

Phew.

You scramble out from under the desk. "Check it out," you whisper. "The handles on the drawers are carved wolf-heads."

"See what's inside!" Corey suggests.

You wrap your hand around the wolf-head handle. "Ouch!" you cry. Something jabbed your palm — hard!

"What happened?" Corey teases. "Did it bite you?"

"Ha ha. Not funny." You examine your hand. Your eyes widen in shock. Your palm is bleeding — from a bite mark!

Turn to PAGE 106.

You struggle to grasp what Corey is telling you. "But why us?" you ask.

Corey shrugs. He looks embarrassed. "I guess they figure kids who put their names on someone else's story deserve what they get."

"Oh." You hang your head.

"Come on," he urges. "We don't have much time."

You grab your parka and follow him to the window. Corey notices that you hesitate.

"This is the best way out," Corey assures you. "We don't want to run into any of them!" He uses your duffel bag to smash the glass. In a flash, he's out the window and sliding down the sheet-rope. You're right behind him.

You glance up. The man in black glares out the window at you.

Go to PAGE 13.

"Look, maybe you scared yourself with this stuff, but I'm out of here." You throw open the closet door and step out. Corey instantly yanks it shut again.

You stroll over to the reception desk and wait. The man in black you saw outside comes down the stairs. He is with a thin woman who has long black hair and pale skin.

"I am Vanessa Rample," the woman says. "Your hostess."

"Congratulations on writing a winning story," the man adds. "And welcome to Twisted Tree Lodge." He bows formally.

They don't strike you as dangerous, just weird. If they both want to dress in black, what's the big deal? You glance past the man and woman to the closet. Corey still hasn't come out.

"Fred will take your coat and bag to your room," Vanessa says. The man in black nods at you. You hand him your coat and bag, and he heads upstairs.

"Room Thirteen," Vanessa calls after him. Then she turns to you. "Come with me and I will introduce you to your fellow writers. They're all having hot chocolate in the study."

"Great!" This weekend might turn out to be fun after all!

If you can keep everyone from discovering that you're a total fake, of course. . . .

Meet the writers on PAGE 21.

You could use some help here. "Okay, which room is Corey's?" you mutter. You wander along the hallway. "Wow," you murmur, "whoever lives here has totally weird taste." Bizarre, gloomy paintings of wolves hang in dusty frames. Ornately carved chairs sit between the dark wood doors. And the carpet! Paw prints are woven in a bloodred pattern.

A sound in the distance makes the tiny hairs on the back of your neck stand up. A long, mournful howl. Then another. And another. This lodge is the perfect location for a horror convention, you think. No wonder Corey was so spooked.

You listen at each of the doors but you don't hear anything. You knock softly on a few. No answer. Is Corey still downstairs in the closet? Did he leave? He seemed pretty freaked out.

You notice Fred, the man in black, dashing down the hall. Maybe he's seen Corey. But that scowl on Fred's face makes you wonder if you should bother him right now.

He's about to turn the corner. If you're going to ask him, do it now.

Ask Fred if he's seen Corey on PAGE 87.
See if Corey is still in the closet on PAGE 99.

You stare at Maria Canto. She turns to face you. You gasp!

She's years younger! Her face is deathly white. And when she smiles, you discover she has two daggerlike fangs.

"We wanted to expand our circle," she explains. "That's why we had the contest. We knew the prizewinners would be like us."

Huh? Your heart pounds hard in your chest as you stare at Grimsy and Wilkes. They transform right in front of you.

Peter Wilkes grows transparent. You can see right through him to the door! And "Grim" Grimsy! Her rotting skin falls off her bones. Her eyes sink into her skull. She looks like one of her own horrible creations.

"Why aren't you transforming?" Grimsy asks, her jaw clacking as she speaks.

"Maybe the moon isn't high enough," Ms. Canto suggests.

"You . . . you're all . . . but . . . you're . . . ," you sputter.

"Why, we are what we write," Grimsy tells you. "Didn't you know?"

Turn to PAGE 27.

You gaze around the terrifying circle. "But I don't understand," you blurt. "Why did you have the contest? And why did we win? We didn't even write those stupid stories."

Corey nods vigorously beside you. Clearly, he's too terrified to speak.

Fred, the man in black, laughs. "That's how we find our victims. We choose kids who put their names on the stories."

"Playtime!" Maria Canto declares. Her fangs hang over her lip as she grimaces at you.

The gruesome creatures circle you and Corey. Your stomach clutches. There has to be something you can do to save your life.

But what?

Think, you order yourself. They keep talking about games — maybe if you play with them, they'll let you live. Or maybe you can get them to turn on one another. You know, divide and conquer.

Whatever you do — do it fast!

Start a game on PAGE 28.
Get them mad at each other on PAGE 82.

You gaze down at the pack of werewolves. Their yellow eyes blaze. Saliva drips from their long fangs.

But they don't climb up toward you.

In fact, they seem to become bored. With an echoing howl, the largest of the creatures leads the others away. They vanish around the corner of the lodge.

"I think we're safe," you tell Corey. "For now."

"Uh, I don't think so," he replies.

Your eyes widen as you watch a giant bat landing on the branch beside you. A vampire bat. "C-C-C-Corey," you stammer.

"I see it!" he gasps.

"And I see you," the bat declares. But the voice is Maria Canto's! She must have turned into a bat to get up the tree.

"You thought you could escape? Well, you thought wrong!" The huge bat picks you up in her enormous claws.

"Nooooooo!" you scream, as the bat drags you away from the tree. It flies you back into the lodge. It dumps you onto the floor.

"Grim" Grimsy, Peter Wilkes, Vanessa, and Fred surround you. In a few minutes the bat returns with Corey. Then it transforms back into Maria Canto.

"We have the little brats," Grimsy declares. "Let the games begin!"

Turn to PAGE 19.

Vanessa leads you into a cozy room. A roaring fire glows in the fireplace. Floor-to-ceiling bookcases line the walls.

Three people sit at a large oak table, sipping from mugs and eating cookies. Vanessa introduces you.

"Come join us!" An old woman with vivid red hair pats the seat beside her. Wow! You recognize her. She's Maria Canto, the author of dozens of vampire books. You sit down.

"So you're one of the contest winners," a man with a gray beard declares. He studies you, as if you were a specimen.

Uh-oh. Could he know that you're a fake? After all, he's Peter Wilkes, a famous mystery writer.

"Wasn't there another winner?" You glance at the blond woman speaking. She's the only one you've never seen before.

She smiles at you. "I'm Stephanie Grimsy."

Your mouth drops open. "Grim" Grimsy? Her books are so scary your mother doesn't let you read them. So you sneak them. She doesn't seem old enough to drive! And she looks so . . . sweet.

"Not what you pictured, right?" she asks with a laugh. "Believe me, I'm the real thing." Her voice drops to a sinister whisper. "There's nothing we hate more than a fraud."

Don't say anything. Just turn to PAGE 33.

"Save them!" the voices cry. You only hope they'll get here in time!

Moonlight streams down through holes in the ceiling. There are pieces of gray flesh hanging off the zombie's face. This creature has no blood flowing through his veins. He is dead and decayed but still moving with the strength of a live human being.

How can this be happening? Your body trembles in terror. Fear zaps your strength. You dangle, horrified, in his grip.

The zombie's bony fingers dig deep into your shoulder. His disgusting face is inches from yours.

The zombie opens his mouth. Oh, no! He's going to take a bite out of your face!

"Hurry!" you scream.

The zombie's teeth are about to close on your cheek.

"Save them!" the voices cry. They rush in behind the zombie.

"Aghh!" You and Corey scream when you see who they are.

Go to PAGE 114.

"I'm going out there to get my bag," you tell Corey. "It sounds as if they're still a couple of floors up. I think I can make it."

Before Corey can stop you, you open the door a crack and slide out. You race over to the bag, grab it, and head back to the closet. The voices are still one flight up. You've got just enough time. You're going to make it!

WHOOOOOOOOOPS! *THUD!*

Your feet go flying out from under you as you slip on a piece of paper. You land flat on your back. The paper flutters down onto your face. You lie there, the wind knocked out of you. Then you peel the paper off your face.

It's the next page of the story.

Turn to PAGE 79.

You step back as the coffin lid rises higher and higher. Until it's open all the way. You hold your breath and wait.

And wait. And wait.

Nothing happens.

You wait some more. Still, nothing happens.

You get up your nerve and tiptoe to the edge of the coffin. You take a deep breath, then glance in. Except for a piece of blank paper, the coffin is empty.

Curious, you reach in.

WHAM! Something knocks you hard from behind. "Oomph," you grunt. You tumble into the coffin. The coffin lid starts to lower.

"No!" you shout. Your scream cuts off in your throat as you stare into a pair of blazing yellow eyes. Corey's eyes!

Only now they are the eyes of a werewolf. Set in a furry werewolf face.

"They got me," he snarls. "And now I must get you."

Just before Corey slams the coffin shut, you glance at the page in your hand. It isn't blank after all. With the last remaining light you read two words. Words that sum up everything.

Come on, you know what those words are.

Yup. The words are

"THE END."

You grab a handful of dirt and throw it in the face of the zombie nearest you. It lands in his open mouth. While he pulls it out with his bony fingers, you grab another handful and throw it at the crowd of zombies.

Corey tears at the dirt too. He heaves great hunks of it into the decaying zombie faces.

"Whoa, check it out," you murmur. The zombies react in a very bizarre way. They pick bugs from the dirt in their open flesh wounds — and eat them! The more dirt you throw, the more bugs they eat. It seems to be a special treat for the monsters.

What are you waiting for? Take advantage of the zombies' snack break!

Run!

Run to PAGE 35.

Your heart pounds hard as you examine the sweatshirt. It's not only torn — it's covered with blood! You peer down at the closet floor. More blood. And coarse tufts of fur.

What happened? And where's Corey?

Is he even still — *gulp* — alive?

Was Corey right? Is something deadly going on here? Was he the victim of some unspeakable horror? The blood, the shredded sweatshirt, and the clumps of fur scattered on the floor make it look as if he was attacked by some vicious animal.

Trembling with terror, you back out of the closet.

And bang into someone.

Turn to PAGE 84.

Your head spins. What is Grimsy saying? You stare at each of the famous writers. Maria Canto is a vampire? Just like the creatures in her stories? She sure looks like one right now.

You glance at the others. That would make "Grim" Grimsy a zombie and Peter Wilkes a — what?

Wilkes notices you staring at him. "That's right," he admits. "I am the ghost of a murder victim. So I write about murder. And to test my theories, I try them out on real people."

Grimsy grins. "After all, it's best to write what you know!"

"For 'The Revenge of the Werewolves' tonight," Canto explains, "we wanted a werewolf with us. To join in the fun. Someone like you."

You tug at your shirt collar. It's getting hard to breathe. These people — no, these *creatures* — think you are a werewolf.

Because of that stupid story! Why did you ever put your name on it?

What should you do? They're waiting for you to transform into a howling half-human, half-wolf monster. Except you know that you won't. Should you confess that you didn't write that story? Or should you keep faking it somehow?

Fake it on PAGE 36.
Confess on PAGE 53.

"Tag, you're it!" you shout. You touch "Grim" Grimsy's outstretched hand. Yeow! She's cold!

You duck under her arm and dash toward the doorway.

A giant bat flutters past you, then hovers in the air. "Nice try," Maria says as she transforms back into a vampire. "But we have different games in mind."

"And we aren't the ones you'll be playing with," Peter Wilkes adds. "No, tonight the werewolves come out to play."

He throws open the window. Three snarling werewolves leap into the room.

Gulp. You better close the book now. You don't want to watch. Because these werewolves look as if they play rough.

THE END

"Maybe we can break through that hole." You point at the small hole above you where the moonlight streams in.

You poke your fingers through the rough hole. You push as hard as you can while Corey pounds the wood, trying to weaken the area. Yuck! Loosened dirt falls into your eyes and mouth. Your fingers strain, but the hole doesn't get any bigger. The wood isn't soft or rotten enough yet to crumble.

"This isn't working," you admit. "Come on. Maybe there's an opening at the other end."

You crawl along the trunk. Corey follows behind you. The only light is the dim moonlight streaming through small cracks. You hope there aren't any snakes or gross bugs under you. You come to a point where the trunk divides into two separate hollow branches.

"Now which way should we go?" Corey wonders.

"I'm not taking any chances," you reply. "This time we'll read the pages first and see what they say we should do."

The first page you take out is smeared with dirt. The only words you can read are: HURRY TO PAGE 97.

Like it says. Hurry to PAGE 97.

Seconds go by. Nothing happens. Blood pounds in your temple. When will he bite? At last you open your eyes.

"Surprise!" a crowd of voices yells. Lights flash on. The vampire releases you. You glance around. The cave is full of people smiling and laughing.

"B-b-but — wh-wh-what?" you sputter. Corey seems stunned.

The man in black steps forward. "Congratulations!" he says. "You two faced all the foes and showed courage at every turn. Welcome to the first Twisted Tree Lodge Horror Writers' Retreat. We proudly pronounce you Honorary Members of the Masters of Horror-Writing Association."

Your favorite horror writers are here cheering for you and Corey! It was all an elaborate game!

"I knew it was fake all along, didn't you?" Corey grins. But he still looks a little pale.

"Uh, sure," you reply. You think over everything that happened. It all seemed so real. And you could swear that the man in black is looking a little hairy. He and his big dog keep sniffing the air. And that vampire's hands were awfully cold — like a dead person's.

Was it all pretend? You'll never know in

THE END.

Those voices coming from upstairs sound too close. You decide not to risk it.

"Just hope they don't notice the duffel bag," Corey whispers.

The voices are even louder now. It's a man and a woman talking, but you can't make out what they're saying. Their footsteps bang on the stairs above you. Beads of sweat form on your forehead. It's hot in this closet.

You peer out the keyhole at your duffel bag. "Don't let them see it," you chant under your breath. "Please, please, don't let them see it!"

You snap your head back when something covers the keyhole.

Someone is standing right in front of the closet door.

Go to PAGE 95.

"A ride?" you repeat. It would be much warmer in the car than out here on this icy road. Still, you know better than to take a ride from a stranger. "I don't think so."

"It's up to you," the woman says. "But you need to be careful. It's a full moon tonight. Not a good night to be out walking."

"Come on," Corey whispers. "She's right."

"Last chance," says the woman. "Are you coming?"

You're still thinking, but Corey answers for both of you.

Go to PAGE 118.

Luckily, before you have to respond, Vanessa makes an announcement. "Dinner will be ready in one hour."

This is your opportunity to avoid any more discussion of fakes. "Uh, I should go up to my room. I just got here. And it was kind of a long trip."

"Of course," Maria Canto says with a smile. "We'll have all weekend to discuss your wonderful story."

That's just what you were afraid of. Maybe you should go find Corey. After all, he's in the same boat.

You take the stairs two at a time. You wander along the second floor, searching for your room. Number 13. Figures.

You wonder which room is Corey's. Maybe you should try to find him. Together you could try to steer the conversation away from those stupid stories.

But you might be better off on your own. Corey seems kind of jumpy. He could make things worse.

If you search for Corey, turn to PAGE 17.
If you go to your room, turn to PAGE 48.

The werewolves' eyes gleam in the moonlight. Several pace back and forth a few feet from the tree. They growl and snap their jaws. They seem furious that they can't get to you.

"The tree!" you murmur. "They can't come close to the tree."

"It must have magical properties," Grimsy comments. "I should put this in a book."

"How can you think about books while our lives are in danger!" Peter complains. "We may have saved ourselves from the werewolves. But now we'll freeze to death!"

You hate to admit it, but he has a point.

"But what can we do?" Grimsy demands. "We can't leave this tree."

She has a point too.

An idea begins to form in your head. "We can't leave the tree," you say slowly. "But maybe we can take the tree with us."

Reveal your plan on PAGE 63.

You and Corey slip away from the zombies. You run farther along the passage. "Hey! I think we can fit through this one." You point to a crumbling hole. You and Corey scurry through.

What is this place? you wonder. You are amazed to discover you're not outside.

"It looks like a subway tunnel or something," Corey guesses. He gazes around at the gleaming white-and-blue-tiled walls.

"Come on," you urge him. "There are stairs up ahead." You race up the stairs two at a time. You realize where you are.

"It's a bus station!" Corey shouts.

"We did it!" you exclaim. "We're out!"

You hurry over to the ticket window. As you reach into your parka to get your money, you pull out another manuscript page. A broad grin spreads across your face.

"We really are safe," you announce. "Now I know for sure." You read him the page: "'Two kids who wander, two kids who roam, at last find themselves on a bus going home.'"

Corey beams. "I can't wait to get out of here."

"Be sure to find out what stop this is," you instruct Corey.

"Why?" he asks.

"Because I want to make sure I never come to Twisted Tree Lodge again!"

THE END

"Uh, yeah, right." Your brain reels. How can you convince them that you really are a werewolf?

"Why hasn't the transformation begun?" Wilkes demands.

"Um." Your voice squeaks, so you clear your throat before you speak again. "Um, you see, I'm a very private werewolf, and I don't like to transform in front of anyone. You understand, right?" You turn to Canto. So far, she seems to be the most sympathetic of the gruesome group.

"Of course. You're still young. A mere pup. You'll get used to it. Go up to your room. Come down when you're ready."

"Thanks!" You bolt from your chair and race out of the room. You take the stairs two at a time.

You yank open your door, then slam it shut. Sweating and straining, you start to move your dresser toward the door.

"Hey," a voice says behind you.

Your heart clutches as you whirl around.

Someone is crawling in through your window!

Turn to PAGE 41.

Your heart pounds as you and Corey sneak out
from under the table. Together you climb into the
closest coffin. You scrunch up as small as you can.
In the tight, dark space you hold your breath and
listen as the vampire stalks slowly down the aisle.

You can hear the vampire snarling and hissing
as he searches for you. "Hungry," he moans.
"Hungry!"

Closer and closer the footsteps come. Any second now, he will walk by your coffin. All you can
do now is hope he doesn't look inside. You wait.
And wait. And wait.

"Hungry!" a deep voice snarls right next to
your ear.

You're too terrified to scream. Both you and
Corey are frozen with fear. Oh, no! The vampire's
fanged face bends over you. And before you can
do anything to stop him, he closes the coffin lid
and snaps the lock shut!

"How easy you made it for me," he laughs. "Two
kids in a coffin. The perfect box supper for a vampire!"

THE END

"Wh-wh-what he wrote," you stammer. "It all came true!"

Corey rushes over to you. You point at the screen. His mouth drops open.

It's all there. The sudden strong wind. The howling outside.

"He made it happen," Corey murmurs. "Just by typing!"

Your head swims. How can this be? How can words on paper come true? But there's the evidence right in front of you. Just like on the manuscript pages that you found outside. Somehow, the man in black either predicts the future or — and this idea makes you shudder — he makes the future come true.

Corey shakes your shoulder. "Snap out of it," he orders. "It sounds as if the werewolves' revenge is starting."

He's right. The howling is growing louder. Now you can hear some distant shrieks.

"The writers!" you gasp. "The werewolves are attacking the writers. Just like the manuscript said!"

"We have to do something!" Corey's voice is tight with fear.

He's right. But what?

Turn to PAGE 101.

"Into the woods!" you shout. "Hurry! Before he catches up!"

Together you dart through the pine trees. You stop when you can no longer see the lodge or the man in black. You lean against a tree and slide to the ground. Corey slides down next to you. He's breathing just as hard as you are.

You rest for a few minutes. You start to shiver from the cold. "We should keep going," you say. "They'll be looking for us."

Corey nods. "Maybe we can find a road." He glances around. "There's a path. Let's follow it."

You and Corey head along the path. "Uh-oh," you murmur.

Footsteps.

You and Corey pick up speed.

So do the footsteps. You look back, but you don't see anyone.

You and Corey duck behind a tree. The footsteps come closer and closer. You peer around the thick tree trunk and gasp.

Silhouetted against the night sky, the man in black stands on the path. And he's not alone!

Go to PAGE 121.

You decide to go after the man in black. You figure he must be one of the horror writers. He'll be worried about losing these pages. Maybe if you give them back to him now, he'll be so grateful he'll give you a reward. Or at least go easier on you if he finds out you didn't really write the prizewinning story.

You dump your duffel bag on the front porch. You stick the pages in your parka pockets and dash around the side of the lodge.

The man is nowhere in sight. "Hey!" you call out. No answer.

You discover a trail of papers. The man in black must have dropped them. You pick the pages up and glance at them.

They don't make any sense — just rhymes and random sentences. No page numbers. Nothing is in any order.

You read the first line on one wrinkled page out loud: "'I'm in big trouble now.'"

"You're not kidding!" a voice from above says.

You peer up at the lodge. A boy about your age dangles from a knotted sheet hanging out a window two floors above you!

"What are you doing?" you call up to him.

"Trying to escape!" the boy replies.

Turn to PAGE 6.

Corey!

The moment he lands, you grab him by the shoulders. "You were right," you cry. "They're all monsters. We have to get out of here."

"I knew this place was freaky," Corey exclaims. "That's why I came back to find you. Now what do we do?"

You pace around the room. "I think we have some time. They're waiting for me to turn into a werewolf." You let out a few howls so they'll think you're up here transforming.

You stop and face Corey. "Hey, you came in the window. We can go back *out* the window."

"Excellent." You and Corey race to the window.

Gulp. Far below you see a sight that chills you. There in the snow are dozens — make that hundreds — of werewolves.

Some are more human than wolf. Some are totally transformed.

None of them looks friendly.

A knock at the door startles you. You and Corey whirl around and stare at it. "Are you all right, dear?" Maria Canto calls.

"Now what?" Corey whispers.

You scan the room. "Out the window. Or hide under the bed."

Maria Canto knocks again. Okay, time's up. Choose!

Head out the window — turn to PAGE 129.
Hide under the bed on PAGE 4.

"Corey, we're *both* in trouble," you whisper. "*Big* trouble."

His eyes widen. He pushes you away from the keyhole and peeks out. His mouth drops open. "What are we going to do?" he whispers.

"The second they leave the lobby we get out of here." You peer out the keyhole again. "Coast is clear. Let's go."

You turn the handle and push on the door. It doesn't move. You try again, your heart pounding. The handle won't budge.

"It's locked!" you exclaim in a hoarse whisper.

Corey tries the handle. After several attempts, he slumps onto the floor of the closet. You slip out of your parka. You slide down next to him, scared and exhausted.

"We're trapped." Corey lashes out an arm in frustration. *WHAM!* He slams his fist against the coats. *WHAM! WHAM! WHAM!*

With the last punch, he hits the wall you're leaning against. A panel slides open! You both fall backwards through it.

"Whoa!" the two of you exclaim.

"A secret passage behind the wall," you declare. "Nice work!"

Head straight for PAGE 50.

Grimsy and Peter scramble out the broken window. They disappear into the dark woods.

You hoist yourself up. You are halfway through the window when a bright light blinds you.

"Stop right there!" a voice orders.

You're so startled, you fall out the window. Before you can get up, four strong hands grab you. They flip you over. You stare up into the faces of two police officers.

"It's just a kid!" one of them exclaims.

"Am I glad to see you!" you cry. Relief floods through you.

"Why were you breaking into the lodge?" the other demands.

"I wasn't breaking *in*," you reply. "I was trying to get *out*."

The two officers exchange a look. "I guess the front door wasn't good enough," the tall one comments. "Come on, move it."

"No problem!" You cheerfully follow the officers to their car. You smile all the way to jail. Behind bars seems like the safest place to be when there are werewolves on the prowl. You wonder if Peter and Grimsy got away.

Months later, you get your answer. "My Night With the Werewolves" by "Grim" Grimsy becomes a best-seller. And it's dedicated to you!

THE END

You grab Corey's arm and duck under the nearest table. You press yourselves flat against the ground.

"Did someone say 'hungry'?" the deep voice repeats.

You peek out from your hiding place and watch a tall, dark figure climbing out of the last coffin. He spreads his cape-covered arms and hisses. His sharp fangs glisten in the sliver of moonlight. His red eyes flash as he scans the area.

"I see the others could not wait for me," he snarls. "But I shall show them all that patience pays off. Why go out to eat when one can so easily have his meal delivered?"

Corey clings to your arm. You feel him trembling. The vampire is heading your way!

"I smell you," the vampire booms. "You will stay for my midnight snack, won't you?" The pale creature strides closer ... closer. He said he smells you, but he still hasn't seen you.

Think fast! Stay under the table? Or sneak into the open coffin nearby?

If you stay under the table, go to PAGE 131.
If you hide in the open coffin, jump to PAGE 37.

You and Grimsy race down the hall. Away from the horror in Maria Canto's room.

How can this be happening? you think. Writers turning into werewolves! Creatures from the pages of horror stories coming to life! If only you hadn't put your name on that stupid story. You wouldn't be trapped in this nightmare!

"We have to warn Peter!" Grimsy shouts. You follow her into the dining room.

Oh, no! You're too late. Peter Wilkes leaps onto the dining room table and lashes out at you with his clawed paws. The werewolves got to him already.

"Run!" you shout. You turn to dash back out the door. Corey blocks your way. Only it's not Corey anymore. He's a werewolf now.

You hear Grimsy shriek as Peter Wilkes pounces on her. You spot Maria Canto behind Corey. They creep toward you. Then lunge!

"Aaaggh!" you scream.

The werewolves will have their revenge.

Which means it's all over for you.

THE END

The zombie pulls himself up, leaves dropping to the ground as he rises. He lifts his arms and reaches bony fingers out to you.

"No!" you shriek. You push the skeletal man back and gasp at the horror of touching his cold, dead flesh. Staring straight into your terrified eyes, he steps forward and grips your neck with one icy hand.

Corey pounces on the zombie's back, trying to pull him away from you. The zombie throws him aside with almost no effort. Corey lands with a thud on the moss-covered ground. He's too freaked to try again. Besides, he's no match for this powerful creature.

"Help! Help!" you cry. Your cries drown out Corey's screams of horror. But other voices call out even louder.

"We're coming!" they shout. "Save them! Save them!"

You feel a glimmer of hope. Someone is coming to save you! Lots of someones!

Go to PAGE 22.

You don't want to take any chances. You grab a page from your parka and read it fast:

"To save yourself from the wolf-man's bite,
Which grows more deadly in the full moon's light,
This piece of paper is all you'll be needing.
Run away now while the wolf-man is reading!"

"What's so interesting?" the wolf-man snarls.

"Here!" you shout, tossing the page on the ground. It flutters in the wind. "Read it for yourself!"

Your trick worked. Just as you hoped he would, the wolf-man chases after the piece of paper. You make a break for it.

"Run, Corey!" you shout. "Run!"

You hurl the walking stick away with all your might. You hope no one ever finds it.

You and Corey race deeper into Lost World Woods. Or at least you think you are heading deeper into the woods. In no time at all, you find yourselves at the very edge of a road!

"Yes!" you and Corey declare together.

Go to PAGE 78.

48

You don't have time to find Corey. You need to get that story out of your duffel bag and read it. Then if the writers have any questions, you'll be able to answer them.

You hurry to Room 13. Once inside, you glance around.

No duffel bag. Where did Fred put it?

You peek under the bed. Nothing but dust. You open the closet door.

"Aaaahhh!" you scream. Two yellow eyes stare back at you from inside the closet.

Corey steps out. Only he looks very, very different.

And very, very deadly.

Turn to PAGE 60.

You open your mouth to speak. No words come out. Only a long, mournful howl.

Corey peeks out from behind a tree. He seems more stunned than terrified. "You're a werewolf!" he repeats over and over again. "You're a werewolf!" He steps out from behind the tree.

You pounce! You sink your teeth into his flesh. He begins to transform. "Yes, I'm a werewolf," you declare. "And now, so are you."

The full moon shines brightly. You howl in unison and then grin at each other. "We better get back to the lodge," you say. "They'll be waiting for us."

"Yes," says your wolf-faced friend. "Tonight is the night that the werewolves take over. And we are the guests of honor!"

Congratulations on winning the horror story contest. Your prize is that you have become werewolves. "The Revenge of the Werewolves" really is your story after all.

THE END

50

"Maybe we'll be able to get out this way," you whisper.

"Or get ourselves in worse trouble," Corey replies.

You wish he hadn't said that.

You move slowly, silently, through the secret passage. The walls are smooth panels of wood. The floor is a highly polished dark wood. It comes to a dead end.

There are two rooms off the passageway. A quick glance into each room shows that they are all furnished with antiques, gilded mirrors, and colorful tapestries.

But no windows. Anywhere. How will you get out?

"Do you think somebody lives back here?" Corey asks.

"Looks that way," you reply. You shudder. "Or they did until the werewolves got them."

"Unless this is where the werewolves live," Corey points out, growing pale. "Come on, let's find a way out of here, fast."

The library has books and a desk. The living room has a big antique trunk in the center. Which room is the best bet for your escape?

If you go into the library, turn to PAGE 96.
If you go into the living room, turn to PAGE 89.

"What happened here?" you murmur. You step into the room. The bedspread lies in shreds on the floor. Chairs are overturned. The dresser mirror is smashed. The curtains are torn off their rods.

Grimsy's face is pale. "A horrible fight took place in this room."

"Or some kind of wild animal was let loose in here," you suggest.

Uh-oh. You hear raspy breathing.

A snarling creature bounds out of the bathroom.

"Aaah!" you shriek. Grimsy grabs your arm. She yanks you so hard you think she's going to rip your arm out of its socket. She pulls you up on top of the dresser.

You flatten yourself against the broken mirror. You stare at the beast. It stares back.

"Maria Canto!" Grimsy gasps.

Turn to PAGE 75.

You whirl around. A boy about your age stands in front of you. He's wearing a green sweatshirt, jeans, and black high-tops.

"Why shouldn't I ring the bell?" you demand.

"You don't want them to know you're here," the boy whispers.

"No, I *do* want them to know I'm here."

The boy's eyes narrow. "Are you one of them?" he asks.

What is with this guy? "One of what? I'm one of the contest winners, if that's what you mean."

"Me too. My name's Corey." His face flushes and he ducks his head. "Only I'm not like you," he mumbles. "I . . . I didn't really write my story. I just put my name on some manuscript I found."

You stare at Corey. "Me too," you blurt.

His mouth drops open. "Really? So we both won a contest with a story we didn't write."

"You know," you say thoughtfully, "even when I tried to confess, no one would listen. It was as if I *had* to win."

Corey nods. "The same thing happened to me. And what a prize! An all-expenses-paid vacation at this freak house!"

You laugh. "It's not that bad," you protest.

"I'm not kidding," he insists. "We're in danger."

Before you can ask him what he means, you hear voices.

"Quick!" Corey grabs your sleeve. "Hide!"

Don't ask questions! Just hide on PAGE 85.

"I didn't write the story," you admit. "I'm not going to turn into a werewolf. I'm a total fake. So go ahead. Tear me to pieces. Do your worst. I give up."

You slump in your chair. You shut your eyes. Funny, even though you're terrified, you actually feel better now that you told the truth.

You hear the three writers burst into laughter. "We know you didn't *write* it," Maria Canto declares.

Huh? Your eyes pop open. Vanessa and Fred have entered. They're both smiling. Your stomach clutches when you notice that Fred has sprouted fur. He's becoming a werewolf.

"Only someone like us would have *found* that story," Fred explains.

What? Is he saying that . . . that . . .

Find out what he's saying on PAGE 59.

You'd rather take your chances with the man. After all, there are two of you and only one of him. "Pick up some rocks," you tell Corey. "We'll fight him off!"

"Right!" Corey replies. He drops down and grabs some stones.

The dark makes it difficult to see your target. But the moment the man is in firing range, you and Corey let loose.

"Yow!" The man throws his head back and howls as one rock hits him on his kneecap.

"Hear him howling?" Corey exclaims. "I told you there were werewolves here. Hit him again!"

You hurl another rock at the man. He ducks, but you fire another round fast. A couple of rocks bounce off the man's heavy jacket.

He throws his arm up to protect his face. "You'll be punished severely for this!" the man declares in a muffled voice. He takes another step toward you. This guy isn't backing off!

"Uh-oh," you cry. "Now he's really mad."

Go to PAGE 91.

Your stomach growls. Maybe Corey will get hungry and show up at dinner. You hear the writers going into the dining room. You head down the stairs to join them.

You glance out the window. The full moon is just beginning to rise through the scraggly tree branches. You hear a mournful howl in the distance. Then another.

You hurry to join the others.

"Ah, our young writer," Maria Canto greets you. "You must be starving. I remember how you young beasts eat."

You sit down beside her and grin. "You're right."

"Grim" Grimsy smiles at you. Peter Wilkes nods politely. You get the feeling he's suspicious of you. Or maybe his face always looks like that.

Vanessa and Fred enter, carrying a plate, silverware, a napkin, and a glass of milk. They place it all in front of you, then leave. You glance down. They've brought you an enormous steak.

Yuck. It looks raw!

Turn to PAGE 117.

There's no way you want to "face your foe." The only way you can think to "open the wall" is to break the window. You pick up your duffel bag, aim, and hurl it at the window.

The duffel bag bounces off the glass as if it were rubber.

HOWWWWWLLLLL! The howling is getting louder. It's just outside your door! The door is creaking open!

You heave the duffel bag at the window again. Again, it bounces back.

"What do you think you're doing?" a furious voice demands from the doorway.

Who's there? Find out on PAGE 133.

"Push hard against the wall!" you order Corey. "Push!"

You ram your backs against the mossy dirt. You grunt with the effort. "Harder!" you shout. "One, two, three!"

The wall falls away! Cold air surrounds you as you tumble backwards through the hole. But you don't hit the ground. Instead you fall through the cold air — and keep falling! There's no ground in sight! Below you is nothing but NOTHING!

The zombies crowd around the hole, watching you fall. The wind rushes by you as you spiral down, down, down. The pages in your parka fly out and swirl around you. Two lines written on a page float before your eyes:

"If the zombies don't get you
NOTHING will!"

THE END

"Okay," you declare. "We'll just leave the pages by the tree and run."

You pull the pages from your parka. You slip them around to the other side of the tree trunk. That way the wolf-man will be sure to see them.

You nod at Corey. Together you creep away as quietly as you can.

"My manuscript!" you hear the wolf-man exclaim.

Great! The plan is working. Once you've put some distance between you and the wolf-man, you stand and run.

Behind you, the dog starts barking and growling.

"Calm down, Igor," the wolf-man says. "We'll have no trouble finding them."

You and Corey pick up speed. You exchange a panicked look.

Uh-oh. What did he mean by that?

Turn to PAGE 72.

Sweat trickles down the back of your neck. Your heart pounds so hard, you think your chest will explode. Your breath comes in gasps. It can't be!

Fred can't mean that you found that story because you're a . . . a . . .

Before you can finish your thought, you raise your head and let out a long, loud howl.

Corey bursts into the room. "What's happening to me?" he shrieks. Fur has sprouted all over his face. His ears have moved to the top of his head and stand up in little points. His nose is elongated into a snout. He covers his wolf-face with heavy paws.

Now you know it's true. It's all true.

Hey, don't take it so hard. Your mom always wonders why you have so many *hair*-brained schemes.

You finally know why!

THE END

"C-C-Corey?" you stammer. "What happened to you?"

He lets out a long howl. "Didn't I tell you we were in danger? A werewolf got me. And now I'm turning into one of them."

"Keep away from me!" you shout.

Corey lunges, his powerful wolf-haunches propelling him across the room. "You wouldn't heed any of the warnings!" As Corey speaks you can see his fangs flashing. Saliva drips from his pointy teeth. Fur continues to sprout all over him.

"What warnings?" You scramble up on top of your dresser.

"That page you found outside," Corey snarls. "That was a warning." He paces back and forth. His claws tear at the carpet.

"You mean about how the werewolves were going to get revenge?" Your heart thuds hard in your chest. You can't take your eyes off the horrifying sight of this wolf-boy.

He howls again. "Yes! To keep the werewolves happy, the keepers of the lodge hold contests." He places his heavy paws on top of the dresser. You scrunch up your toes. "And they plant those stories. They bring cheaters up here. Cheaters like us!"

"B-b-but why?" you stammer.

Corey sits back on his haunches. "Because kids are so tasty!"

Turn to PAGE 107.

You read Side Two with a trembling voice:

> " 'With one winner gone, you stand alone
> And soon you'll face your foe.
> The writer's dream of a night of fear
> Comes true and soon you'll know
> What evil lurks in shadows gray
> Where howling signals doom.
> Now you must choose: Open the door
> Or open a wall of the room.' "

It sounds as if the writer is writing to you! Is it the man in black? How could he have known that one winner would be gone and you'd be left alone? This page seems to be predicting the future. Like those first pages that told about winning the contest.

Is this page trying to tell you what you should do right this minute?

OW . . . OW . . . HOWWWWL!

Howling! It's out in the hallway! Is it the howling that "signals doom"?

Turn to PAGE 123.

"H-h-how can this be?" you stammer, glancing down at the pages. How can anyone know all this and put it into a story?

If the author knows the past, you wonder if he knows the future too. You frantically turn to another page in the story:

"They're all doomed! Everyone at the lodge will be destroyed. Just as writers destroy the werewolves and other creatures of the night in every horror story written! Those who write or read of horror and fear shall face those same horrors and fears. Tonight will be 'The Revenge of the Werewolves'! And the only ones who will know this story are the one who wrote it — and the one who reads it now."

Turn to PAGE 8.

"Break off some branches," you instruct Grimsy and Peter. "If we carry them, maybe we'll be able to keep the werewolves away."

"Sounds good," Grimsy says. She snaps off a branch.

"Sounds crazy," Peter mutters. He gazes at you. "I think before we all risk our lives, you should test your theory."

You stare at him. "Fine," you declare. "I'll check it out first." You use all your strength to break off a thick branch from the twisted tree. Grimsy hands you another one. You shove it into your pocket. You take a deep breath and move away from the tree.

Within seconds the werewolves surround you.

You hear the ragged panting of the beasts. You smell their sweaty odor. The stench of their animal breath. They creep closer.

You can't stand it! "Stay back!" you scream. You shut your eyes and lash out with the branch.

Turn to PAGE 67.

"Whoa!" you cry. You fall a few feet. You land on a moss-covered dirt floor. Corey tumbles beside you.

"I think we're out of the tree trunk," you comment. You lie on the ground catching your breath. You stare up at a dirt roof.

Corey leaps to his feet. "Get up!" Corey shouts at you. "The ground is moving!"

Corey's right! The ground is shifting underneath you! You try to stand, but your feet keep slipping on the wet moss and leaves.

A face bursts through the dirt. Just inches from yours.

"Ahhh!" you scream. You gaze into the hideous face of a monstrous man. Rotting flesh hangs off his cheekbones. His blank eyes stare straight ahead. A disgusting odor rises from him. He's more skeleton than man. He shouldn't be moving.

But he is.

Go to PAGE 46.

"Get inside!" you whisper. "Maybe if they can't see us, they'll give up." You and Corey crawl into the giant tree trunk. The air inside the cramped space is thick with the musty smell of rotting wood. A spongy, green moss covers the walls, ceiling, and floor. You crawl away from the entrance.

"It's hard to breathe in here," Corey complains. "I hope we don't have to stay too long."

"At least it's warm. We'll just wait a little while until we're sure we're safe," you assure him.

You wait until you think the wolf-man has passed. Then you crawl back toward the entrance.

A huge boulder blocks the hole!

"Push it away!" you exclaim. You both throw your shoulders against the boulder. It won't budge.

"We should have followed the advice from the manuscript!" you cry. "It told us not to come in here."

You and Corey stare at each other as the truth sinks in.

You're trapped inside the giant rotting tree trunk!

Go to PAGE 29.

"If we can make it to that tree," you declare, "I think we'll be safe."

"Run right to the werewolves?" Peter yells. "Are you insane?"

"Well, you can take your chances with whatever got Corey and Maria Canto," you respond. "But I'm out of here." You glance at Grimsy. "How about you?"

She nods. "Peter, we have to try to get to the tree." She grabs one of his arms and tugs. He rises shakily to his feet.

For a guy who writes terrifying murder mysteries, he sure is a wimp, you think.

"Okay, on the count of three, I'm going to open the door," you tell them. "Run as fast as you can for the twisted tree." You gaze at them. "Ready?"

"Ready," Grimsy replies.

"Ready," Peter whispers.

"One. Two. Three!"

Race to PAGE 71.

"Keep away!" you shout again. You blindly wave the branch.

THWACK! You hit something.

Your eyes pop open. And widen in amazement.

The werewolf you hit begins to transform. You watch as the wolflike features change — back into Corey!

You reach out with the branch and touch another werewolf. It howls when you make contact. Then it starts becoming human.

"The tree branches turn them back into people!" you shout.

Grimsy dashes beside you. Together you poke and prod the werewolves. You glance behind you. Peter still cowers at the tree.

"Thank you!" a half-wolf, half-man creature cries. "You saved us!"

"They've been under a curse," Corey explains. "The werewolves wanted revenge on horror writers. And kids who read horror stories. So they held contests. They planted stories for kids to find. That's how they decided who to bring here to turn into werewolves."

"But you've broken the spell!" Maria Canto exclaims. She still has thick fur. "The werewolves have been defeated."

You and Grimsy beam at each other. You did it! Your plan worked. And the werewolves' revenge has at last come to an

END.

68

You decide to open the door and face your foe. Gathering all your courage, you slip your fingers around the doorknob. You take a deep breath and give it a hard twist.

Oh, no! You forgot that you're locked in! You release the knob. Your eyes widen in horror as you see the knob turning by itself. Someone is on the other side, opening your door!

You dart to the bed, jump under the covers, and pretend to be asleep. It sometimes works with your parents. Through squinting eyes, you watch the door creak open.

Your heart pounds when you see the long black cape approaching the bed.

"Get up!" a voice whispers. "We're getting out of here!"

Go to PAGE 73.

"Fine," you tell Peter. "Ask them what they've done with Corey." As if they're really going to tell you, you add silently.

You and Grimsy follow Peter out to the lobby. He steps up to the reception desk and hits the little bell.

You wait a few minutes but no one comes. "This was a great idea," you mutter.

Peter glares at you. He rings the bell again.

You glance behind the desk. "Yikes!" you exclaim. "What are those doing there?" You point down to a pile of bones. Gross. The bones have bits of flesh clinging to them.

Peter peers over the counter. His face grows pale.

"Still think this place is normal?" you demand.

"Uh-oh," Grimsy says. She's standing in front of a computer terminal at the other end of the desk.

You join her. You glance at the computer screen. She's reading an E-mail message.

And the news isn't good.

Turn to PAGE 116.

You stare at the werewolf — too stunned to speak.

He paces around the lobby, growling. "That's a perfectly good ending. What's wrong with it?" he demands.

Corey bursts out of the closet. "Too obvious!" he shouts.

The werewolf glares at Corey. "What do you mean?"

"What you've written is, like, so predictable," Corey explains. "I mean, you write it, it happens, so where's the surprise?"

Even though Corey sounds like he knows what he's talking about, you can tell he's really scared. But his plan to distract the werewolf seems to be working.

Uh-oh.

He may be having luck with *this* werewolf, but a dozen more beasts are now slinking into the lobby. . . .

Now what?

Turn to PAGE 120.

You yank open the door. You dash outside. Pumping your arms, you hurl yourself across the lawn. Snow crunches under your feet.

Oh, no! The werewolves' heads whip around in your direction. Faster, you urge yourself. You're almost there. You pick up speed.

Yikes! A growling, snarling werewolf leaps toward you. It misses. Your lungs burn. You've never run so fast in your life!

You fling yourself at the twisted tree. *OOOMPH!* You land facedown on a gnarled root. Peter grabs a low branch. Grimsy collapses against the trunk.

You roll over and sit up. You lean against the tree. "Made it!" you gasp.

Panting and trying to catch your breath, the three of you stare into the darkness.

Hundreds of werewolves stare back.

Turn to PAGE 34.

You and Corey duck behind some bushes to hide. You glance back toward the wolf-man and his howling hound.

And gasp!

A trail of manuscript pages leads directly from the wolf-man to your hiding place!

"B-b-b-but I left the pages at the tree," you sputter.

The wolf-man laughs. A really mean laugh. "You may have left them," he says, his voice a rasping growl. "But they didn't leave you."

"But how — " you start to ask.

He cuts you off. "This is my story!" He rattles a page at you. His claws puncture the paper. "If I want something to happen, these pages make it come true!"

He takes another step closer. You can smell his foul animal breath. You stare at the paper he waves in front of you. You see that instead of words, it's covered with little arrows. Pointing at you and Corey!

Face it. There's no escape. You and Corey are only characters in the werewolf's story. And your parts in it have come to a grisly

END.

Your eyes pop open. Standing at the foot of the bed is the boy you met outside!

"What are you doing here?" you exclaim. "I thought you left!"

"I couldn't just leave you here. Not after what I saw. I snuck back in and got the key from behind the front desk. Hurry! They'll be coming for you any minute."

"Who?" you ask.

"The werewolves. This place is crawling with them."

You stare at him. "Werewolves? Are you crazy?" you exclaim.

"No, I'm Corey Mackenzie. And I know you're the other winner. Only I didn't really write my story. And I bet you didn't, either."

"How did you know?" You stare at him. "I found it."

"I found mine too. It's all part of the werewolves' revenge. They planted the stories for us to find. They staged this bogus contest to lure the writers here."

Your mind reels. Can this all be true? "But why?"

"They're mad at horror writers and horror readers. They claim they get a bad rap. They want to turn us all into werewolves."

Your mouth drops open. This is unbelievable!

Go on to PAGE 15.

You and Corey exchange confused glances. He gazes around the lobby. "What's going on here?" he asks. "It looks like a waiters' convention."

He's right. The lobby is filled with dozens of waiters. Old, young, men, women. All wearing waiters' uniforms and name tags.

You peer at the name tag the waiter in front of you wears. Your eyes widen in shock. You recognize that name. It's the name of a very famous horror writer.

You glance down at your printout.

Oops.

You're not a good typist. You typed the word *waiters* instead of *writers*. So now all the horror authors are waiters.

"May I show you to your table?" the waiter-writer asks. "After all, you are the guests of honor."

The waiter leads you and Corey into the banquet. You smile as you realize that you got into this mess by pretending to be a writer. But you saved the day by becoming one.

Now, if only you had remembered to spell-check!

THE END

She's right! Maria Canto's blue eyes peer out of a face sprouting fur. Red hair is still piled on top of her head.

But she's not human anymore. She's halfway between woman and wolf. She has powerful, fur-covered haunches and sharp fangs. She still has arms, but instead of hands she has paws. She lets out a loud howl as her torso shudders and twists. She's turning into a werewolf in front of your terrified eyes.

"Get out while you still can!" she screams. "Don't let this happen to you! They're after us! All of us!"

"But why? Who?" Grimsy asks. She still clutches your arm. You feel her trembling as much as you.

"The werewolves," Maria Canto responds. "They hate us — the horror writers and horror readers. They hate that we profit from their misery. This is their revenge. To kill us and turn us all into werewolves." More fur sprouts on her face.

"What should we do?" Grimsy wails.

But Maria can no longer answer. She throws her head back and howls. She is all werewolf now.

"Let's get out of here!" you cry. You leap off the dresser and run out of the room. Grimsy is right behind you.

Turn to PAGE 45.

"If something's in those coffins," you whisper, "it's not anything I want to come face-to-face with! Let's keep going."

"Whew!" Corey breathes a sigh of relief. "I was hoping you'd say that."

You tiptoe past the long rows of coffins. If there is anything inside them, it doesn't seem to care whether you stay or go. So you just keep going. Before too long you actually see a pale light shining up ahead.

"We're almost there!" you cry excitedly. "Yes! We're going to make it!" You hurry to get to the end. And when you and Corey finally come to a big opening where moonlight streams down brightly on a clearing in the woods, Corey shouts for joy.

"We made it!" he cries.

Cheer all the way to PAGE 78.

"The werewolves are hanging around the front," you comment, "so let's go out the back."

Peter and Grimsy follow you to the kitchen in the back of the lodge. One glance tells you Grimsy was right — no back door.

You peer out the window. "We should head for those woods."

"We can hide and plan our next move," Grimsy agrees.

You grab a chair. "I'll smash the window. The noise may attract attention, so be ready to move fast."

"I can't believe this is happening," Peter moans.

"Well, it is." This guy is getting on your nerves. "Deal with it!" You raise the chair over your head. And throw!

SMASH! The chair crashes through the window. Shards of glass fly everywhere.

A loud bell starts ringing.

"We tripped an alarm," you shout. "Get out, now!"

Turn to PAGE 43.

You come to the same icy road that brought you into this nightmare. The bumpy mountain road the bus traveled along. In the distance, the lodge looms above you. "Great!" Corey exclaims happily. "We made it!"

"Not yet we didn't," you reply, remembering the terrible bus ride. "It's a long way down the mountain."

You trudge down the mountain road in silence. You shiver. It would sure be nice to have a ride right now, you think.

No sooner do you think the thought than two headlights come down the road. A car pulls up alongside of you. The woman driving rolls down her window and speaks from the darkness inside the car. "May I offer you two kids a ride?" she asks in a friendly voice.

If you take the ride, go to PAGE 118.
If you say no, go to PAGE 32.

"No!" you cry. You're so afraid, you can't get up. You read the terrifying text:

"Going for the duffel bag wasn't the first stupid mistake the kid made. Oh, no. The first stupid mistake was pretending to write the prizewinning story. So now the kid lies flat on the floor in Twisted Tree Lodge. Listen! Do you hear the howling? The footsteps on the stairs? The werewolves are coming! With flashing fangs and blazing yellow eyes, the Night of Revenge begins now!"

You fling the paper to the ground. Why bother getting up? You know every word is about to come true. You hear the howling. You can even smell the sweaty odor of a wild, vicious beast.

A werewolf races down the stairs. It lunges at you. Its yellow eyes blaze and its fangs flash. Just like in the story.

You dodge and roll out of its reach. The werewolf crouches, ready to attack again.

"This can't be the way it ends," you wail. You pound the paper on the floor.

The werewolf freezes. It cocks its head to one side. "Why not?" the creature demands. "What's wrong with that ending?"

Huh?

Go on to PAGE 70.

You and Corey decide to follow the advice on the page. "The dog won't be able to pick up our scent in water," you tell Corey.

You step into the icy water and start wading downstream. You stay close to shore, to take advantage of the cover of the thick bushes that line the sides.

You hear the dog's barking echo through the forest. From the sound of it you can tell that the dog stopped where you and Corey went in the water.

"It worked!" Corey exclaims. "I think we lost him!"

"You may have lost the dog, but you didn't lose me!" the man in black bellows from the edge of the stream.

Terror grips you. There's no getting away from him now.

"But the manuscript!" you cry. "It told us to go into the stream."

The man laughs. "Fool! I *wrote* that manuscript."

You smack your forehead. Of course he'd know exactly where you'd go. You were doomed the moment you picked up that story. Right from the very beginning. Which is why this is

THE END.

"We need these pages," you insist. "Let's go."

You and Corey take off running. You hear the wolf-man and his dog behind you. Luckily you and Corey have a head start. You lose them for a few moments.

You come to a shallow stream. Lying next to the stream is a huge hollow tree trunk. Even on its side, the tree is almost as tall as you. And it's so long, you can't see the other end of it.

"Now what?" Corey asks.

"I say we start using these pages to help us survive." You pull out a page and read it to Corey:

> " 'When faced with the choice
> Of tree trunk or stream,
> Go into the water
> Or prepare to scream!' "

"It can't be any clearer than that!" you exclaim. "I guess we should go into the water."

"We'll freeze," Corey argues. "And that moon is so bright he'll find us again in no time if we don't hide somewhere. I think we should ignore that stupid manuscript. Let's keep going."

What will you do?

Wade into the stream on PAGE 80.
Crawl inside the tree trunk on PAGE 65.
If you keep running, run to PAGE 132.

"So, who gets us as the prize?" you ask. "After all, there's only so much of us to go around." You hope if they have to compete for you, they'll start fighting each other.

"What?" "Grim" Grimsy turns her hollowed-out eye sockets toward you in a zombie stare.

The creatures stop advancing. Could your plan be working?

"Well," you continue. "Zombies eat flesh. But vampires drink blood. So there's a problem right there."

"What are you doing?" Corey whispers in horror.

You ignore him. "And you murder people," you say to Peter Wilkes. "But there are only two of us. So someone has to lose out. There just isn't enough of us for everyone."

You watch as the zombie, vampire, and ghost eye one another. Your heart pounds harder. What will they do?

"Fool!" Maria Canto sneers. "We are great friends. Share and share alike. We wouldn't ever let anything as silly as a pair of kids come between us."

What terrible luck. You and Corey are trapped by an incredibly reasonable group of monsters.

Well, it's nice to know that even ghouls have best friends.

Too bad it means your

END.

Your sudden attack catches Corey by surprise. "It's me!" Corey cries, scurrying away from you. "Why are you hitting me? I'm your friend!" Corey ducks, just escaping another hard hit.

Your arm feels as if it's being pulled out of its socket.

Corey darts behind a tree.

"Come back!" you shout after him. "It's not my fault. It's the stick!"

The bearded man appears before you again. To your horror, he begins to transform. Terrified, your eyes widen as the old man changes into a werewolf!

Go to PAGE 124.

"Aah!" you yelp.

"I'm sorry!" "Grim" Grimsy apologizes. "I didn't mean to scare you. I didn't see you coming out of the closet."

"Th-that's okay, Ms. Grimsy," you stammer.

"Call me Grim. Everyone does. Have you seen Maria Canto?"

You shake your head. "Why?" you ask.

"I heard strange noises in her room," she explains. A worried expression clouds her features. "But when I knocked on her door there was no answer. And I can't find her anywhere."

"Really?" Now there are two missing people at the lodge.

Another wolf howl pierces the night. Grimsy shudders. "I don't know about you, but this place gives me the creeps."

You glance around. "I think we may be in danger here," you whisper. "The other contest winner tried to warn me and now . . ." You hold up the ripped sweatshirt. "I found this in the closet. He was wearing it the last time I saw him."

Grimsy's eyes widen. "What should we do?"

Hey! That's what you were going to ask her!

Go to PAGE 109.

Corey pulls you into a closet built under the stairs. He shuts the door, and you are plunged into darkness. You feel coats and heavy clothing hanging around you.

Now you can ask questions. "Why are we hiding?" you whisper.

"I heard one of them talking," Corey explains. "He said the real horror story was about to begin."

You snort. "That doesn't necessarily mean anything." You shake your head. You can't believe that you let this guy spook you. You start to turn the door handle. Corey stops you.

"I'm serious. This whole contest thing is some kind of scam," Corey declares. "I know it sounds crazy. But we have to stay hidden until we can figure out what is going on around here."

You peer at Corey's face. It's hard to see in the dark. Is he playing some kind of weird joke? Or does he actually believe the stuff he's telling you? Maybe you should just ignore him and go check in, you think.

What's it going to be? It's getting hot in this closet! Make up your mind.

If you decide that Corey is wrong, leave the closet on PAGE 16.

If you decide to stay hidden, turn to PAGE 98.

You decide to go into the lodge. The woods look too dark and scary. And the boy has already disappeared from sight.

"Come around to the front!" the man calls to you again. "And be careful of those pages! They're my whole future!"

So he really is one of the writers. These pages must be from his next book. Too bad they don't make any sense, you think. You stuff the pages into your parka and dash around to the front.

As you approach the porch, you're surprised to see a woman with long black hair grabbing your duffel bag. "Hey!" you shout. "That's my stuff!"

"That's all right, dearie," the woman replies in a low, raspy voice. "I'm bringing it inside for you. Come in. We've been waiting for you!" You follow her into the lobby of the lodge. "Sign in, please," she instructs you, pointing to a large black book on the reception desk.

You are about to write your name in the book when you spot a name on the line above: COREY MACKENZIE.

The name has been crossed out.

Go to PAGE 137.

"Hey, Fred," you call. You jog toward the man in black.

He whirls around. "What is it?" he demands.

Whoa. Maybe this was a bad idea. He seems really mad that you stopped him. But now that you have, you better hurry up and ask your question.

"Um, I was just wondering. Have you seen Corey?"

"Who?"

"You know, the other kid winner," you explain.

"Never heard of him," he responds. He spins on his heel and darts around the corner.

You stare after him. "That was weird," you mutter. Why would he claim he didn't know Corey? Doesn't he greet all the guests as they arrive?

"Dinner!" Vanessa calls from downstairs.

Time's up. Time to face the writers.

Turn to PAGE 55.

"Hey!" you cry. "Why are you locking the door? Hey!"

"It's for your own safety," the man replies from the hallway. "We're not locking you in. We're locking others out. Don't worry. I'll come back for you soon." Before you can respond, you hear him walk away.

That boy was right! Something terrible is going on here!

You hurry to the window to see if you can open it. No such luck. It's nailed shut. When you glance down you discover a sheet dangling from the outside sill. This is the room the boy escaped from. Only now those creepy people have made it escape-proof.

You need to come up with a plan. You take off your parka and fling it onto the bed. A paper flutters to the floor. The man in black missed a page.

You notice writing on both sides. Your head snaps up when you hear footsteps. You have to hurry! Which side will you read first? To make up your mind quickly, you toss the paper up in the air and read the side that lands face up!

Toss this book in the air. If it lands front cover up, turn to PAGE 11.

If it lands back cover up, turn to PAGE 61.

"The living room," you decide. "Maybe there's something useful in that trunk."

"I'll meet you there," Corey tells you. "I'll scope out the library. We'll save time that way."

"I don't know if . . ." You're about to say you don't know if you should split up, but he's already ducked into the other room.

You shrug and enter the living room. "Mistake!" you exclaim. You wrinkle your nose in disgust. What a stench!

The black velvet chairs and bloodred sofa have been shredded. A big cat — or *something* — has been using the furniture as a scratching post. Thick tufts of animal fur cling to the fabric. You pick up a tuft and rub it between your fingers. You've never seen fur like this. It's coarse and oily.

"Corey, wait in the library," you call over your shoulder. "This place stinks." You toss down the fur.

You can't resist taking a quick look in that trunk. You cross to it and discover something surprising. It isn't a trunk.

It's a coffin!

If you open the coffin to see what's inside, go to PAGE . . . Never mind, you don't have a choice. The coffin is opening by itself!

Quick! Get over to PAGE 24!

"Don't touch it!" Corey warns. "It might be a trick."

"It's just a stick." You shake your head, shrugging off Corey's warning. You take a step closer.

"That's right," the old man agrees. "A stick can't do you any harm. Here. Take a look."

You take the stick from him. Your fingers start tingling. An electric shock crackles through your veins. Your body shudders with a powerful force. You feel heat shooting through you.

It must be coming from the stick! You try to throw it down. But you can't! It's as if it's stuck to your fingers.

"Help!" you cry. "Get this thing off me!"

You glance around, but the old man has vanished!

Corey grabs a heavy tree branch. *WHAM!* He smacks the head of the walking stick with all his strength. The impact sends you reeling backwards.

Suddenly, the walking stick comes alive! Orange lights flash from the wolf's eyes. The beast opens its mouth and exposes sharp fangs, dripping with foamy drool. The wolf-head turns toward Corey.

With a power totally out of your control, the walking stick swings your arm back and forces you to strike Corey!

Go to PAGE 83.

"Hold your fire!" the man shouts angrily. "You're in enough trouble already."

"Hey, wait a minute." You drop your handful of rocks. "That guy's voice sounds familiar."

"No way!" Corey blasts you. "Then you're hanging out with the wrong crowd!" He backs away from you. "You're one of them!"

"I'm serious." You peer into the darkness, trying to get a better look at the man. "Dad?" you call out.

"Dad!" Corey exclaims. "You mean that — that monster is your dad?" He's totally freaking out.

The man catches up to you. It's your dad, all right. And even in the darkness you can see he's annoyed. This could be bad.

"The contest people called," he says. "They told me to come and get you because you didn't really write that story. They said the same was true of this young man. You kids should be ashamed!"

"B-b-but, Dad," you sputter. You try to explain about the werewolves and the man in black.

"Haven't you told enough stories?" your father responds angrily. "Now march straight to the car. I'm taking you home. All I can say is, I hope you've learned your lesson!"

Hmmm. Maybe it would have been less scary to go into the woods than to be in this much trouble with your dad.

THE END

Terror floods through you. Searing pain rushes along your muscles. Your limbs twist uncontrollably. Sweat pours off you. You feel as if you're burning up.

"What is happening to me?" you scream. But all you hear is a tortured howl.

"No!" Corey gasps. His eyes are wide with horror.

Your nostrils fill with his scent. Your mouth waters. You let out an enormous roar and lunge at him.

"Ahhhh!" he shrieks, and stumbles backwards into the dresser.

You catch a fleeting glimpse of yourself in the dresser mirror as you hurtle by. You are stunned by your reflection.

Your face! You've sprouted fur. It's patchy, but it's there. And your hands have become paws with long, deadly claws.

You are transforming into a werewolf.

That desk handle really bit you and passed on the werewolf curse.

The manuscript page was true — every word. Tonight is the werewolves' revenge. It begins in this room, with you and Corey. And once your dreadful work is done here, you will join the rest of the werewolves of Twisted Tree Lodge. Forever. Because for you, life as a kid has come to a very twisted

END.

"Right is right," you whisper. "Let's go!"

With the dog's furious barking echoing through the trunk, you crawl right. Sweat drips into your eyes. But you can't rub them because your hands are covered in dirt.

"Yikes!" Corey yelps behind you.

Your muscles tense with fear. "What?"

"Sorry. Didn't mean to scare you," Corey says. "A bug just ran across my neck. Gross."

You keep crawling. You feel as if the sides of the trunk are squeezing in tighter. You breathe in the musty, thick odor. It smells damp and rotten.

Is there enough air in here? you wonder. Will we suffocate before we find the way out? You start struggling for air.

You keep moving forward. You can already tell that your knees are going to be badly bruised. You reach out with your scratched-up hand and place it down.

Onto nothing.

Turn to PAGE 64.

Corey reaches into the car and grabs a handful of manuscript pages. Together you work furiously to rip each page into a million pieces. And with every page you destroy, something amazing happens.

The man in black, vampires, werewolves, zombies, mummies, and mutants flatten into paper-thin figures. With every page torn, another monster falls to pieces.

At last you hold up the final manuscript page. The page that tells how the story ends. You smile victoriously when you read:

"Two conquered the horrors the writers write.
Two survived all the hits that they took.
But the true winners are the readers who know
To end horror just finish the book!"

Yes, you think to yourself. It's time to end the horror. It's time to finish the book. With that, you tear the last page into the tiniest pieces of all. And stepping through the pile of shredded monsters and conquered fears, you and Corey walk shoulder to shoulder into the lodge and call home.

THE END

What are they doing? You squint through the keyhole again, but it's still covered. Have they discovered your duffel bag?

You can hear footsteps as someone walks around the lobby. "Hey, what's this?" you hear a man say.

Your heart sinks. Great. They must have found it.

You hear a zipper and then a gasp.

"What is it?" the woman asks. She's the one standing in front of the door.

You hear paper rustling. "The kid read this," the man replies. "The whole plan for tonight's revenge. Our plan to attack the writers and the readers of horror." His voice sounds like a low growl. "Now what do we do?"

"Nothing stands in our way," the woman announces. "We don't want the child warning anyone. So we'll just have to make sure that child never speaks to anyone. Ever again."

Gulp. Turn to PAGE 122.

"Let's check out the library," you tell Corey. "Maybe the books will give us some idea of what's going on here."

"Or how to escape," Corey says.

You enter the library and notice something standing in the corner. Something familiar.

Hanging on a wooden coatrack is a long black coat, a black hat, and a black briefcase.

"Corey," you exclaim, "I think I know who lives back here."

"Is this good news or bad news?" Corey asks.

"I'm not sure. Remember that manuscript page I found?"

Corey nods.

"It fell out of that briefcase." You point to the coatrack. "And the briefcase was carried by a man wearing that coat."

Corey gazes at the coatrack. "Okay, but who is he? That story was all about werewolves getting revenge. So, is he one of the famous horror writers? Or is he a werewolf?"

You shake your head. "I don't know. Maybe — "

Footsteps in the hallway! Corey ducks behind a curtain and flattens himself against the wall. There are only two possible places left for you to hide.

The footsteps are right outside the door! Hurry!

If you hide under the desk, turn to PAGE 14.

If you wrap yourself in the long coat, turn to PAGE 112.

When you find page 97 you read out loud as fast as you can:

"'Who sleeps in a darkened moss-lined bed?
The ones not living yet not dead.
Whose fangs are sharpest? Who's worse to fight?
Vampires left or zombies right.'"

"Vampires and zombies?" Corey gasps. "What kind of choices are those? If we go right, the zombies will eat our flesh. If we go left, the vampires will drink our blood!"

"What kind of place is this Lost World Woods?" you moan. "How did we get into all this trouble?"

"More important, how do we get out of it?" Corey points out.

You hear something that makes your blood run cold. Barking!

The dog caught your scent! The man in black must have rolled aside the boulder. Because the barking is coming from inside the tree trunk!

"Hurry!" Corey gasps. "Left or right?"

If you're left-handed, go left to the vampires on PAGE 111.

If you're right-handed, go right to the zombies on PAGE 93.

You have to admit, everything about this contest so far has been really weird. Corey might be right. Maybe there is something dangerous going on at this lodge.

You release the doorknob, and you hear Corey sigh with relief.

"Did they say anything else?" you ask.

Corey gulps. "That tonight was the night for revenge. Everyone at the lodge will be destroyed."

Your heart starts to pound hard. Aren't those practically the same words on that manuscript page you found outside?

"Corey," you blurt. "I found part of a manuscript and a bunch of it already came true. And one page predicted that werewolves were going to get revenge here, tonight."

Could those have been werewolf voices you heard? You peer out the keyhole. The lobby is still empty.

"Oh, no!" you gasp.

"Do you see a werewolf?" Corey's voice is tight with fear.

"No, my duffel bag," you reply. "It's still out there."

Now what? Should you take a chance and try to get the bag? Or should you stay where you are and hope no one notices it?

If you decide to grab the bag, turn to PAGE 23.
If you stay put, turn to PAGE 31.

You don't want to bother Fred. He seems really distracted. You hurry downstairs to see if Corey is still hiding in the closet.

You knock softly on the closet door. "Corey?" you whisper.

No answer. You turn the knob and open the door.

Empty. Well, the closet is full of coats, but no Corey.

You notice a pile of rags on the floor. That's weird, you think. These weren't here before. You reach down and pick them up. And gasp!

You're holding Corey's green sweatshirt. And it's been ripped to shreds!

Turn to PAGE 26.

You don't want Peter Wilkes stirring things up. "You're right," you tell him. "It's probably all just my imagination."

"Now you're sounding more sensible," Peter responds.

You hold up the sweatshirt. "I'm going to put this in my room." You catch Grimsy's eye. You give her a tiny nod. She nods back.

You hurry to your room. A few minutes later Grimsy rushes in.

"That was just an act for Peter, wasn't it?" she says.

"Yes," you admit. "I don't want Fred and Vanessa to know we're suspicious."

"Good thinking," Grimsy replies. "No wonder you won the story contest. You think like a horror writer."

You figure this isn't the time to confess. "Let's check out Maria Canto's room. Maybe we'll find something that will tell us what's going on."

Grimsy leads you to Maria Canto's room. She knocks but there's no answer. She tries the door. It opens with a long, slow *CRE-EE-EAAK*.

Your eyes widen in shock. The room is totally trashed.

Turn to PAGE 51.

You stare at the computer screen. As if somehow the words on it can save you.

"That's it!" you exclaim. "If I erase what he wrote, the attack will stop." You are about to hit the DELETE key when another idea occurs to you. "Or maybe I should change what's here. You know, rewrite it."

"Well, do something quick," Corey urges. "I hear footsteps."

Your fingers hover over the keyboard. The howling and screams grow louder. And heavy footsteps are thudding closer.

Hit the DELETE *button and head for PAGE 126.*
Start typing on PAGE 103.

102

The car pulls up at the lodge. A crowd of vampires, werewolves, zombies, mummies, and hideous mutant creatures of every shape and size are standing out in front.

"Last and only stop, Twisted Tree Lodge," the vampire announces. "Get out!"

A ghoulish figure with flesh hanging from its bones opens the car door. It gestures to you and Corey to come out. Corey climbs out first. You're about to follow when you glance down. Lying on the floor is another page from the manuscript. You squint to read in the darkness:

"The story is only as real as it seems.
Horror is only horror in dreams.
Destroy all the pages one by one.
The story ends when the last page is done."

You know what to do! You yank the pages out of your parka and start ripping them to shreds one by one. "Corey!" you cry. "Help me kill the story! Tear up the pages!"

Go to PAGE 94.

Your fingers fly across the keys. Please let this work, please let this work, you chant silently.

If the man in black can write the future, you hope you can too!

As you tap out the words, the screaming stops. And instead of deep, terrifying howls of rage, you hear tiny little yips.

"It's working!" you cry. "I wrote that all the werewolves turn into little poodles. And that the writers are safe."

"Awesome!" Corey cheers.

You grin. "And that the two kids are heroes." You leap up from the chair. You and Corey slap high fives.

You hit the print key, then grab your rewritten version of the story. You and Corey dash downstairs.

A large banner hangs over the reception desk. It reads WELCOME, HEROES! The lobby is filled with little yappy dogs.

A man in his thirties wearing a crisp white apron approaches you. "May I help you?" he asks.

"Yes," you reply eagerly. "Where are the writers?"

The waiter looks puzzled. "What writers? There are no writers here."

Huh?

Turn to PAGE 74.

104

You decide to check the coffins to make sure they're empty.

"Help me open this one." You move over to the next coffin in the line. Slowly, carefully, you and Corey lift the lid a little. You feel your heart pounding. "See anything?" you whisper.

"It's too dark inside," Corey replies. "We have to lift the lid higher." A loud creaking sound sends shivers up your spine as the lid finally falls open all the way.

"Empty!" you exclaim, breathing a huge sigh of relief.

One by one you and Corey open the coffins and find the same thing in each one. Nothing. There's just one coffin left at the farthest end of the line. "One more and we're done," you announce. "Maybe they keep these coffins for the lodge guests who don't survive the lodge food!" you joke.

"Oh, don't even mention food," Corey moans. "That reminds me how hungry I am."

"Did someone say 'hungry'?" a deep voice asks from the end of the row. You peer down the aisle to where the last coffin rests on the table. To your horror, the lid is opening all by itself!

Quick! Turn to PAGE 44.

"Oh, man," Corey moans. "It's not a cave — it's a tomb! This place is full of coffins!"

"Shh!" You put your finger to your lips. "Just keep walking. There must be a way out. After all, they had to get them in here somehow."

You tiptoe down the aisle that separates the two long rows of coffins.

"This is too creepy!" Corey whispers. "Who's inside all these things?"

"I don't know and I don't care," you declare. "As long as it's not us! That's all that matters."

The tiniest bit of moonlight shines through the ceiling like a laser beam. You strain your eyes to see where you're going. Corey follows close behind you. Too close. He trips and falls forward, pushing you against one of the coffins!

CRASH! The coffin tumbles down from the table and falls to the floor. You scream as the lid of the black box creaks open!

Go to PAGE 119.

"Um, Corey, I think it *did* bite me," you say.

Corey snorts. "Come on, it was a joke. You probably just got a splinter. Now help me look through these boxes."

You have to sit down. You feel really weird. All tingly inside. Your head feels full of cotton.

"Maybe we can find a weapon or a tool," Corey is saying, but his voice sounds very far away.

What is wrong with me? you wonder. You can't remember ever feeling like this before. Your skin itches, and you feel your fingers and toes flex and unflex. You can't control it.

"Hey! One of these boxes is full of keys. Maybe they'll open the closet!" Corey turns and looks at you. A concerned expression crosses his face. "What's up? You look funny. And you're shaking."

You grunt a reply. Maybe you're getting sick.

Your eyes lock onto Corey's. Your mouth waters. For some reason, gazing at him makes you hungry.

Fear enters his eyes. "Are you okay?"

Are you? Turn to PAGE 92.

The room spins. Terror makes you dizzy. Your knees buckle and you slide off the dresser to the floor.

Corey pounces on your chest. He breathes his horrible wolf breath into your face. It feels as if he's crushing the air out of you.

"Then I tried to warn you," Corey declares. "But, no — you didn't believe."

"I believe! I believe!" you gasp.

"Too late. Too late for you. Too late for the writers. The werewolves shall have their revenge. Just as it was written."

And just as it is written, you have now come to

THE END.

108

"What are you doing?" you cry. You and Corey are thrown against each other in the backseat. "We don't want to go up the mountain. We want to go down!"

Now that you're heading this way, the full moon hangs low in front of you. The light shines directly into the car. In the rearview mirror you finally get a glimpse of the driver. Her eyes burn deep red. Her skin is ghostly pale. Bloodred lips only partially cover a pair of gleaming fangs. The driver isn't an ordinary woman. She's a vampire!

"Didn't anyone ever tell you never to take a ride from strangers?" she hisses, speeding up the road. "You are the guests of honor. You must come and accept your award for the best horror story!"

"But I didn't even write the best horror story!" you cry.

"Me, neither!" Corey adds.

"Oh, but we didn't want you to *write* the best horror story. We wanted you to *live* it! Don't you see? The real horror is just beginning. And the story cannot end until we put an end to you!"

Go to PAGE 102.

"I don't know what to do," you reply.

"Let's go in to dinner," Grimsy suggests. "Maybe Maria will show up. And we can ask Peter Wilkes what he thinks of all this."

You and Grimsy enter the dining room. You discover Peter Wilkes sitting alone at the table.

"Peter," Grimsy declares, "we think we have a problem."

Peter raises an eyebrow. "Oh?"

Grimsy urges you forward. You explain about Corey's warning and disappearance. As you're talking, you remember the manuscript page you found outside. The one that said that tonight the werewolves were going to get their revenge.

It all fits together! The wolf-head door knocker. The wolf paintings. The paw-print rug. The howling. The shredded, bloody sweatshirt. You gulp. "I think Corey may have been attacked by a . . . by a . . . by a werewolf!" There. You said it.

Peter Wilkes bursts out laughing.

Control your anger and turn to PAGE 127.

The boy ducks behind a huge boulder. You're left standing alone in plain view.

"There you are!" The man in black calls down to you from the window. "I see you found my manuscript. Great! I really need those pages. Bring them around to the front, will you?"

"Don't do it," the boy whispers from his hiding place. "Your only chance is to get away now."

"Come on inside!" the man shouts. "It's getting dark. I'll meet you at the front door and let you in! I want those pages."

"Trust me!" The boy crawls toward the woods. "You don't want to go in there!"

Trust him? You just met him!

Still, the kid seems genuinely afraid. Could his story be true?

You gaze up at the window. From where you're standing, you can't tell if the man in black has claws or regular old fingernails.

Tough choice. Should you follow the kid into the dark, spooky woods? Or should you go into the lodge and face the mysterious man in black?

If you go into the lodge, turn to PAGE 86.

If you follow the boy into the woods, go to PAGE 130.

You're left-handed so you go to the left. You and Corey move forward in silence. You don't hear the dog anymore. He must have given up and gone home. And you and Corey are too scared to talk. You know that somewhere up ahead are deadly vampires.

To your surprise, the hollow tree branch opens into a large cave. Figures. Where else would a bunch of vampires hang out?

"Now what?" Corey asks.

His voice echoes in the high chamber. Hundreds of sleeping bats awaken and swoop down around your head!

"Corey! Look out!" you shriek in terror as you duck and swat at the vicious bats with your hands.

"I see them! I see them!" he hollers back.

The flapping of wings creates a windy roar. But the bats are the least of your worries.

Lined up along the moss-covered walls are two rows of coffins.

Go to PAGE 105.

112

You peek through the huge coat and see a large man dressed in black. He backs into the room, pulling a wheeled cart. You can't see his face, but you're almost positive it's the same man you saw outside. The man who dropped the pages.

Whatever the man is dragging, it must be heavy. He's huffing and puffing. He pulls the cart over to you and stops it right in front of the coatrack. In front of you! You try not to breathe. You hope your feet are well covered.

The man pulls a cloth from the cart, uncovering a computer. He starts it up and begins typing. You hear a powerful wind whistle outside. Then terrifying howls. The man chuckles softly.

A noise distracts him. He gets up and steps out of the room. *WHAM!* Somewhere down the passageway, a door slams.

You wait a few minutes. He doesn't come back.

You creep out of the coat. "It's okay, Corey," you whisper. "All clear."

Corey slips out from behind the curtains. He pokes his head out the door. "The hallway is empty."

"Good." You sit at the computer. "I want to see what he was writing."

You glance at the screen and gasp!

Turn to PAGE 38.

"Take the stupid old stick!" you shout at the yellow-fanged wolf-man. "Just take it!" You try to throw it at him, but the stick clings to your hand! It seems to have a will of its own.

"Give me my stick!" The wolf-man growls angrily.

"I'm trying to give it to you!" But the stick won't leave your hand! The more you shake it, the harder it stays stuck.

The wolf-head glows again. A bright light flashes from the wolf-head's eyes. It nearly blinds you.

Suddenly you see, hear, and smell things more clearly than ever before. The more you shake the stick, the more alert your senses become. You just don't feel like yourself at all. You touch your hands to your cheeks and feel fur. Your knuckles are even hairier than your grandfather's!

Something drastic is happening here. But what?

Go to PAGE 49.

"More zombies!" you shriek.

Dozens of the walking dead emerge from the shadows, surrounding you and Corey. They don't want to save you from the zombie. They want the zombie to save you for them!

The dead, rotting monsters move in closer and closer. You grip the dirt wall and prepare to be devoured by the zombies.

A piece of dirt comes off in your hand, leaving a hole in the wall. If you keep digging the dirt away, maybe the hole could be made big enough to crawl through.

You think fast. Should you throw the dirt in their rotting faces? Or should you push harder against the wall and hope an even bigger hole opens?

The choices are both rotten, but they're the only ones you have!

If you throw a handful of dirt in the rotting faces of the zombies, turn to PAGE 25.

If you push against the rotting wall and hope you can escape through a hole, turn to PAGE 57.

It's the boy from the lodge! But he's not a boy anymore!

He's a werewolf!

"I knew you'd follow me," the wolf-boy gloats. "They all do. They all fall for that 'escape while you still can' act." He laughs. At least you think that snorting, growling sound is a laugh.

"Who falls for it?" you ask.

"Horror fans," he replies. "That's why the contest winners are such easy pickings. Because they think all this stuff could actually happen."

Your head swims. "B-b-but it is happening," you stammer.

The werewolf shrugs. "Hey, sometimes you get lucky. And, my friend, this is your lucky day."

You crawl away from the terrifying creature. He lashes out and grabs your ankle. You can feel his claws through your jeans.

"Yup, this is the day you get to live one of your favorite horror stories. The one that won you the contest. 'The Revenge of the Werewolves.'"

He smiles, baring long yellow fangs. He's going to turn you into a werewolf. And that means this is one story that is never going to

END.

116

You read the E-mail message aloud:

" 'It's all set. The contest lured the writers just as you thought. Those stories we planted at different schools brought us the required children. The werewolves will be pleased tonight.' "

"Still think I'm making this up?" you ask Peter.

"We're doomed!" Peter wails. He collapses to the floor.

Great, you think. He's going to be a *big* help.

You dart to the front window and pull back the heavy curtain. The full moon illuminates a terrifying sight. Huge wolves — werewolves — heading toward the lodge.

"Check the back," you instruct Grimsy. She dashes out.

"I don't want to die," Peter moans.

"Me, neither," you snap. "Get a grip."

Grimsy rushes back in. "I didn't see any werewolves. But it's so dark I can't be sure. And there's no back door."

"How can we escape?" Wilkes asks.

You notice something strange. The werewolves avoid the giant twisted tree out front. Maybe there's something about the tree that they don't like. But can you get to the tree before the werewolves get to you? Or should you sneak out the back?

Try for the tree on PAGE 66.
Go out the back on PAGE 77.

You wait a few minutes for the others to be served. You figure you'll ask Vanessa or Fred to cook your steak a little longer when they bring the other dinners. But no one comes back into the dining room.

"The service here isn't too good, is it?" you joke.

"Grim" Grimsy gazes at you, puzzled. "What do you mean?"

You shrug. "Shouldn't they bring you your food?"

The writers exchange amused glances. "That's a good one," Maria Canto chortles.

"Grim" Grimsy pushes her pink headband farther back on her head. "As if we ate dinner." She giggles.

"But you should eat," Peter Wilkes urges. "And hurry. The fun is about to begin. You'll need all your strength."

"What fun?" Have they planned activities? Corey should be here. He's going to be disappointed that he missed the games. "What do I need my strength for?" You smile expectantly.

Maria Canto rises from the table. She crosses to the window, where the full moon gleams. "For 'The Revenge of the Werewolves'!"

Uh-oh. What's going on here? Find out on PAGE 18.

118

"Yeah!" Corey says. "Thanks! That would be great!" Before you can stop him, Corey opens the back door and climbs into the car.

"It's a cold night to be out on the mountain," you hear the woman say to Corey.

"Sure is," Corey replies. He motions for you to get in.

Well, she sounds friendly enough. And it really is freezing out here. You climb in next to Corey. "You're right. It's freezing out there. Thanks for the lift."

You shut the door. Instantly, the woman steps on the gas pedal. The car starts slipping and sliding on the steep icy road.

"Slow down!" you cry. "It's too icy to go so fast!"

The woman ignores you. Instead she goes faster and faster. So fast that the car spins completely around. You're no longer heading down the mountain.

You're heading back to the lodge!

Go to PAGE 108.

"A vampire!" you cry. You jump away from the open coffin.

You stare in horror for a few seconds. Finally you realize there is no vampire. The coffin is empty!

"Why would anyone keep a bunch of empty coffins out here in the middle of the woods?" Corey whispers.

"We don't know they're *all* empty," you reply. "The manuscript page said there were vampires in this branch of the tree. So the vampires are either in these coffins, or they went out."

"You mean they went out for a bite?" Corey laughs nervously.

"Ha ha." You roll your eyes. "Vampires are night creatures. They drink blood at night and sleep all day. In *coffins*!"

"So maybe we're safer in here than outside," Corey suggests. "Maybe we should just stay in here until daylight comes."

You shiver. "Or maybe we should check to make sure all the coffins really are empty," you whisper.

"You're kidding, right?" Corey says. "Open them *all*?"

He may have a point. "We have no idea when the vampires will come back," you admit. "It seems to me we have two choices. Get out of here now or check the coffins and stay here until daylight."

Keep going on PAGE 76.
Open the coffins on PAGE 104.

"People like surprise endings, twists, you know," you declare. You hope that having this totally bizarre conversation with a pack of werewolves will somehow save your life.

"Hmmm. You make a good point," the first werewolf says. Some of the other werewolves nod.

A huge, powerful creature sits up on his haunches. You wouldn't want to get on his wrong side. "All of the other writers had really stupid suggestions for improving our stories."

A small werewolf beside you leans in close. "So we eliminated them."

Gulp.

Go to PAGE 125.

The man in black is pulled forward by a huge dog on the end of a thick leash. Both the man and the dog sniff the air in all directions.

The man takes a few steps in your direction. You and Corey press yourselves flat against the tree trunk and hold your breath.

Seconds seem like hours. You wait. And wait. And wait. Until you feel as if your lungs will burst.

Go to PAGE 135.

"Sounds like you're in trouble," Corey murmurs.

You put a finger to your lips. Is he crazy? The woman is still standing right in front of the closet.

Luckily, she didn't hear him. She moves away from the door. Now you can see into the lobby.

Only you wish you couldn't. Because the guy discussing your fate isn't a guy!

The heavyset man paws through your duffel bag — with paws!

Thick tufts of hair rise from the top of his head, and you realize those are his ears. His hairy face isn't a man's but a wolf's. You clutch the doorknob to keep from falling over in shock. The man in black is a werewolf!

He's a monster! A monster created by horror writers.

Only he's real!

Turn to PAGE 42.

OW...OW...OWWWWL! The howling is getting closer to your room. Sweat beads up on your forehead.

You read Side Two again, hoping for a clue. What should you do? "Open the door," you mutter. "Or open one wall of the room. How am I supposed to do that?"

You run your hands over the walls of the room, searching for an opening. Nothing! No secret panel. No hidden door. The only opening in the wall is the window! You'd have to break it to escape and now it's almost dark out. Where would you go?

"Calm down. Calm down," you murmur. "Think! Think!"

You hear footsteps just outside your door. In a few seconds it will be too late to decide anything. Hurry!

If you decide to "face your foe," open the door on PAGE 68.

If you decide to "open the wall," break the window on PAGE 56.

The wolf-man bares fangs that could snap you in half in one bite. "It didn't work!" the creature howls. "I thought if I got rid of the stick I would be rid of the werewolf curse. But look at me!"

"I'm looking! I'm looking!" you assure the werewolf.

"Give me the stick!" the creature growls angrily, as he circles you. "Only with the stick can I have a few precious hours as a normal man. Without it, I am doomed to this form always."

You feel the power of the stick weakening. The wolf-head returns to its wooden form. The stick is just a walking stick again.

But you know the stick has tremendous power. And you have no idea what the werewolf will do if you give it back to him. He might attack you as soon as you hand it over. Maybe you should consult the manuscript. But do you have time? The werewolf is looking impatient!

If you give the stick to the wolf-man, go to PAGE 113.

If you hold him off long enough to read a page from the manuscript, go to PAGE 47.

"Will you stay and help us fix our stories?" the huge werewolf asks.

You and Corey glance at each other. He raises an eyebrow. You shrug. After all, do you really have a choice?

Since you and Corey are total horror fans, you know what makes a good story. The werewolves are excellent students. In no time at all, several werewolves publish best-selling horror stories.

You and Corey enjoy your time at Twisted Tree Lodge. Of course, it can be a little hairy at times. The pressure is always on.

For you and Corey it's edit . . . or else!

THE END

THE END

(Well, what did you expect? You deleted everything. The werewolves, Twisted Tree Lodge, the whole story. Including you and Corey. So it's time to shut the book now. It's all over. Actually, now that you erased it all, the story never began.)

"My dear child." Peter chuckles. "Your imagination has run away with you. Grimsy, I'm surprised at you. Encouraging this."

"But you don't understand — " you cry.

"Nonsense," he cuts you off. "This is a horror conference. You are a horror fan. It would be only natural for you to imagine any number of things. But it's all just make-believe."

"I don't know," Grimsy protests. "The disappearances concern me. Where is Corey? Where is Maria Canto?"

At least Grimsy is still on your side. "Yeah, and what about this?" You hold up Corey's sweatshirt.

"Why don't we simply ask the proprietors?" Wilkes suggests. "Perhaps they can shed some light on this mystery."

You're not sure you want to do that. What if Vanessa and Fred are behind everything? You want to keep searching for Corey. Or maybe just get out of there — while you still can!

Still, Wilkes could be right. There could be an explanation for all of this.

If you agree to talk to Vanessa and Fred, turn to PAGE 69.

If you insist on keeping quiet, turn to PAGE 100.

The man in black glares at the woman. He stuffs the pages into his coat pocket. He grabs your duffel bag. "Up to your room, now," he orders. He nudges you ahead of him up the stairs.

"Forget the pages," he mutters. "Ha! The pages are the only thing that matter."

"So," you begin, nervously trying to make conversation, "are you one of the writers?"

"Not *one* of the writers," he replies angrily. "*The* writer! The only one who knows how to create real horror and make the pages come to life!"

"That must be hard to do," you respond. This guy has some ego! Still, you want him to calm down. He seems to get mad awfully easily. "You must be really good."

"Or really *bad!*" the man in black bellows. He snickers at his own joke. He pushes you toward a room with an open door. He shoves you inside.

Tossing your bag onto the bed, the man in black tells you to make yourself comfortable. He shuts the door — and locks you in!

Go to PAGE 88.

"Quick," you whisper. "Out the window."

You and Corey dash to the window. A large tree stands outside. A thick branch brushes against the ledge. "That's how I got up here," Corey tells you.

"Then that's how we'll get down." You grab on to the branch. You crawl along until you are close to the trunk. Corey creeps behind you. You reach out with your leg and swing around to the other side. You don't want Maria to see you if she peeks out the window. Corey understands what you're doing and swings onto a branch below you.

But you're not safe yet. Not with the snarling, howling werewolves below you.

Cling tight and turn to PAGE 20.

130

You decide to follow the boy into the woods. The lodge is giving you the creeps. And you don't like the way that guy in the window is glaring down at you.

You head for the woods. That was where that boy was going. "Hey!" you call out. "Where are you? Wait for me!"

No answer.

"Great," you mutter. "Now what do I do?" These woods are awfully spooky. You shiver as you glance around at the dark, twisted, and gnarled trees. Anything could be hiding in them.

Something jumps you from behind!

"Aaaaah!" you scream. You hit the dirt with a grunt.

You lash out, twisting and turning, trying to get out from under the beast that sits on your back. You can hear it panting in your ear. It lets out a low growl. Somehow you manage to break free from its grip. You roll away and glance over.

And your eyes widen in horror.

Go to PAGE 115.

"Don't move!" you whisper to Corey. "Maybe he won't see us."

You lie down and try to flatten yourself against the floor. You never knew how bulky your parka was until now. The padding makes it difficult to get really flat. Then you realize the padding isn't in your way. The manuscript pages stuffed down the front of your jacket are.

You reach in and pull out the wrinkled bundle.

"Look!" Corey gasps. He points to the balled-up page on top of the pile. "It's glowing!"

You unwrinkle the page. The words on the page are written in glow-in-the-dark ink!

Then you read what they say.

Turn to PAGE 134.

"Run!" you cry. "Deeper into the woods. Away from the path."

You leap over branches. You dash under tree limbs. Corey follows you through the dark forest. Finally you come to a stop, gasping for air.

"I don't hear them," Corey says. "We must have lost them."

"We lost us too," you admit. "I have no idea where we are."

"Perhaps I can be of help," a crackly voice declares.

You jump as a bearded man carrying a walking stick steps out from behind a tree. He looks old and frail.

"Who are you?" you demand. "Are you from the lodge?"

"The lodge? No! No! They won't have me." The man laughs. "I'm just a nature walker, that's all. I know every stick in this forest. If you're lost in Lost World Woods, I can lead you out. Follow me."

"Look at his walking stick," Corey whispers.

Your eyes open wide. It's got a wolf-head handle! The eyes, the fur, and the fangs are all carved in perfect detail.

"Made it myself," the old man declares proudly. "Take a closer look." He holds the stick out to you.

You reach for it.

Go to PAGE 90.

The woman from the lobby glares at you. She holds a large, howling dog on a leash. "How dare you behave like a little vandal!"

She stalks into your room and picks up the phone. "We are sending this child home," she barks into the receiver. "Immediately. We can't wait for the bus. Call the van." She hangs up and turns to you. "Gather your belongings and wait in the lobby."

You do as she says. You can hear her muttering about your bad behavior while you wait for the van. You're beginning to feel like a total wimp. You let your imagination run wild.

One by one, the famous horror writers arrive. Only you're not going to get a chance to meet them. Well, you won the contest by faking it. So being sent home in disgrace is kind of the ending you deserve.

THE END

"Where you are hiding, the vampire knows
As soon as he sees this page that glows!"

How could you be so stupid? you scold yourself. The glowing paper will attract the attention of the vampire. He'll know where you're hiding!

You ball up the glowing page and stuff it back into your jacket. But it's too late. The vampire must have seen the light under the table. He crosses to you in a flash.

Your heart pounds. There's no way to escape. You're trapped with Corey under the table. The vampire bends down and with each powerful hand grabs you and Corey.

The vampire drags you both out from under the table. He lets out a vicious hiss. You stare into his mouth and your stomach curdles. His fangs already look a little bloodstained.

You squeeze your eyes shut and wait for him to dig his fangs into your neck.

Go to PAGE 30.

The man shouts orders to the dog. "Find them! *Find them!*"

You know you can't hold your breath much longer. Just when you think you'll explode, the man and dog take a few steps in the other direction. You and Corey let out your breath.

"That dog is going to pick up our scent," Corey whispers.

"We have to do something fast," you agree.

The dark clouds roll away. A full moon shines down from the black sky. You press yourselves tighter to the tree, hiding from the moon's bright light. You hear a bloodcurdling howl.

"Wow," Corey murmurs. "What kind of dog is that?"

You can't help yourself. You have to peek around the tree.

"It's not the dog howling!" you gasp. "It's the man!"

Turn to PAGE 12, if you dare!

The man in black grins. "Hey, cheer up," he tells you. "You shouldn't have any trouble coming up with the best list. After all, you're a good writer. You wrote one of the winning stories."

He shuts the door.

You stare down at the paper in your hands. Your mind goes blank. As blank as the page. You can't think of a single thing.

Write, you order yourself. Or else! You start your list:

"Why I Should Be a Character in This Story."

1. I'm the number one horror fan.
2. I'm really good at finding weird hiding places.
3. I think werewolves, vampires, and zombies are way cool.
4. My mom says I have an earsplitting scream.
5. Almost nothing grosses me out.
6.
7.
8.
9.
10.

Uh-oh. That's all you can think of! And there are still blank spaces on the list.

Oh, well. You knew writer's block was bad. But you never thought it would be the cause of your

END.

The woman notices you staring at the name in the book. "Corey Mackenzie," she sneers. "He was here under false pretenses."

"False pretenses?" you repeat. "What's that?"

"He didn't really write his winning story," the woman replies. "So we separated him from the rest. Only genuine masters of horror may participate in this gathering. I'm sure you agree."

You gulp. You hope she doesn't find out that you didn't write your winning story, either. "Did you send him home?" you ask.

"Let's just say he's been taken care of," the woman answers. An evil smile crosses her face.

What does that mean? you wonder.

The man in black appears at the top of the stairs. "Do you have the pages?" He doesn't even give you time to answer. He dashes down the stairs and reaches into your parka.

"Hey!" you cry. He sure is pushy!

He pulls out a handful of pages. "Did you get all of them?"

"I . . . I . . . I think . . . ," you stammer.

"Forget the pages!" the woman interrupts. "We've got work to do!"

Things are getting strange. Maybe they'll be less weird on *PAGE 128.*

About R.L. Stine

R.L. Stine is the most popular author in America. He is the creator of the *Goosebumps, Give Yourself Goosebumps, Fear Street,* and *Ghosts of Fear Street* series, among other popular books. He has written nearly 200 scary novels for kids. Bob lives in New York City with his wife, Jane, teenage son, Matt, and dog, Nadine.

GIVE YOURSELF Goosebumps®

...WITH 20 DIFFERENT SCARY ENDINGS IN EACH BOOK!

R.L. STINE

❏ BCD55323-2	#1	*Escape from the Carnival of Horrors*
❏ BCD56645-8	#2	*Tick Tock, You're Dead!*
❏ BCD56646-6	#3	*Trapped in Bat Wing Hall*
❏ BCD67318-1	#4	*The Deadly Experiments of Dr. Eeek*
❏ BCD67319-X	#5	*Night in Werewolf Woods*
❏ BCD67320-3	#6	*Beware of the Purple Peanut Butter*
❏ BCD67321-1	#7	*Under the Magician's Spell*
❏ BCD84765-1	#8	*The Curse of the Creeping Coffin*
❏ BCD84766-X	#9	*The Knight in Screaming Armor*
❏ BCD84767-8	#10	*Diary of a Mad Mummy*
❏ BCD84768-6	#11	*Deep in the Jungle of Doom*
❏ BCD84772-4	#12	*Welcome to the Wicked Wax Museum*
❏ BCD84773-2	#13	*Scream of the Evil Genie*
❏ BCD84774-0	#14	*The Creepy Creations of Professor Shock*
❏ BCD93477-5	#15	*Please Don't Feed the Vampire!*
❏ BCD84775-9	#16	*Secret Agent Grandma*
❏ BCD93483-X	#17	*Little Comic Shop of Horrors*
❏ BCD93485-6	#18	*Attack of the Beastly Babysitter*
❏ BCD93489-9	#19	*Escape from Camp Run-for-Your-Life*
❏ BCD93492-9	#20	*Toy Terror: Batteries Included*
❏ BCD93500-3	#21	*The Twisted Tale of Tiki Island*
❏ BCD21062-9	#22	*Return to the Carnival of Horrors*
❏ BCD39774-5	#23	*Zapped in Space*
❏ BCD39775-3	#24	*Lost in Stinkeye Swamp*
❏ BCD39776-1	#25	*Shop Till You Drop...Dead!*
❏ BCD39997-7	#26	*Alone in Snakebite Canyon*
❏ BCD39998-5	#27	*Checkout Time at the Dead-End Hotel*
❏ BCD40034-7	#28	*Night of a Thousand Claws*
❏ BCD40289-7	#29	*Invaders from the Big Screen*
❏ BCD41974-9	#30	*You're Plant Food!*
❏ BCD46306-3	#31	*The Werewolf of Twisted Tree Lodge*
❏ BCD39777-X	Special #1:	*Into the Jaws of Doom*
❏ BCD39999-3	Special #2:	*Return to Terror Tower*
❏ BCD41920-X	Special #3:	*Trapped in the Circus of Fear*
❏ BCD43378-4	Special #4:	*One Night in Payne House*

$3.99 EACH

Scare me, thrill me, mail me GOOSEBUMPS now!

Available wherever you buy books, or use this order form.

Scholastic Inc., P.O. Box 7502, Jefferson City, MO 65102

Please send me the books I have checked above. I am enclosing $_____ (please add $2.00 to cover shipping and handling). Send check or money order—no cash or C.O.D.s please.

Name _____Age_____

Address _____

City _____State/Zip _____

Please allow four to six weeks for delivery. Offer good in the U.S. only. Sorry, mail orders are not available to residents of Canada. Prices subject to change.

GYG498

SCHOLASTIC ❖ PARACHUTE